DRAGON'S PRICE

Rise of the Horned Serpent–Part 1

DANIEL POTTER

FALLEN
KITTEN
PRODUCTIONS

Chapter One

Few remember the moon; her pale beauty lives only in ancient words and artists' dreams. Yet everyone knows who murdered her.

— SEEK FIRE, CHIEF OF THE TURTLE
CLAN OF THE LOW RIVERS TRIBE,
LOREKEEPER

THE WIND'S GENTLE WHISPERINGS TURNED TO screeching howls in the ears of Captain Madria, known as the Silver Fox. She stood on the rear deck of her ship and home, *Fox Fire*, grimacing as she listened to the wind's complaints. The hull groaned as the headwind seized the ship and changed the timber of the steady *whup whup whup* of her twin propellers as they clawed their way forward. Madria whispered a prayer before locking the twin levers in place. They jutted from the deck on either side of her, each one corresponding to a propeller. Both were as far forward as

Madria dared without stressing the ship's power crystal. Turning to her right, she opened a few drawers in a cabinet that was bolted to the deck.

The deck boards creaked and Madria glanced up at her first mate, Swallowing Hawk. At nearly eight feet tall, the woman towered over everyone and everything. Madria had never met anyone taller who had claimed to be human. She was muscled like a mountain lion, and the woman's eyes radiated with cold rage.

"He's coming for us," Hawk said, her words falling like stones.

Madria could not help turning to scan the bank of gray clouds that receded behind them. "We don't know that. The east wind does not need a reason to be angry."

Hawk said nothing as Madria pulled out two incense pellets. savory and saffron to calm the east wind, honeysuckle and clover to entice the west wind to their aid. With a prayer to the winds, she struck a match.

A sudden gust snuffed the flame. Madria bit back a curse. She spoke into the wind. "It's not a person. It's a dragon. He doesn't count." The wind clawed at her lips and eyes as the ship strained to make any forward progress.

"Oathbreaker." The single word sliced past her ears.

"Funny time to notice that now." Madria hissed at it before turning her back on the east wind. Sheltering another match with her body, she lit the sweeter incense for the west wind.

With the incense trailing a line of thick smoke, Madria placed it in the metal tray on top of the cabinet. Hawk had turned toward the clouds, searching it with the largest spyglass they possessed. "There he is. Six o'clock. Should I tell the crew?"

"That will serve zero purpose." The constant blowing over the bow of the ship slackened as the colder eastern wind caressed her neck. Eddies of air grasped at her skirts as the two winds began to battle. Madria lit a second incense pellet in thanks as *Fox Fire* resumed its forward momentum. "They'll do what they must. Let them and my children enjoy a few more hours of the open sky." She stepped away from her post. "You have the helm."

Hawk smoothly took her position, gripping the levers with two fingers each. Madria felt her first mate's eyes on her back as she walked to the front of the poop deck to a well-cared-for shrine. Three bright red timbers framed two wooden screens, a torii, a gate to the sacred. As she undid the latch, she heard the giant woman issue a derisive snort, a noise that eerily reminded her of an ill-tempered horse Madria had been tasked with as a child.

Ignoring her, Madria opened the shrine, revealing the wooden figure of Coyote, the moon eater, curled in a sleeping position, one ear pointed outward. In front of the figure sat three smaller ones: a Fox, her coat streaked with silver gray, a rhinoceros bearing a golden horn, and a white flower that radiated its purity. Madria knelt before the figures, her hands pressed together. Hawk's eyes burned like a mutinous dagger in her back. No one understood. The stories went that Coyote had destroyed the world of humankind. Handed it over first to the gibbering madness and then the greed of the dragon emperor. In the Golden Hills, he was akin to the Yozi. Among Hawk's people, the Low Rivers Tribe, he represented power unbowed to responsibility. Asking for his help would invite ruin. Yet the spurned god rarely refused her entreaties; few were brave enough to even utter his name.

Coyote, show me the way forward. She prayed, opening her mind and calling out for him. At once, she heard the echo of his laughter mixed with a howl that cut through her heart. With a start, her eyes snapped open. The wooden Coyote

3

had lifted its head and was looking directly at Madria, ears back. First, the Rhino wobbled and fell on its side, then the Flower. Both figurines lay more still than inanimate things could ever be. Only the Fox stood.

"No." Madria snarled, curling her lip back in a feral expression. Reaching in with both hands, she righted the figurines. "No one can have them, not even you."

The little fox smoked and then burst into a bright orange flame. Madria snatched the figure from the shrine and snuffed it out.

"Then so be it." Madria spat the words at the shrine as she stood. She closed it without putting the Fox back in. Her tear-rimmed eyes caught Hawk's as she turned. "When I give the order, you get them both off this ship, you understand?" she commanded with a bitter sharpness.

Hawk hesitated only to blink once before nodding. "I will do my duty."

Chapter Two

To stand on the Spine and look east is to see the Seven Saved Lands. Before Dragons, before the cities were planted, as consuming darkness flowed up the rivers, seven gods spared humanity from their own folly. White Buffalo, All-Father, Black Otter, Daylight, Tree Mother, Blind Owl and the Seventh who makes his bed in the bones of that day. Together, they united the will of the world against the dark.

> — SEEK FIRE, CHIEF OF THE TURTLE
> CLAN OF THE LOW RIVERS TRIBE,
> LOREKEEPER

ISHE LEANED OVER THE BOW OF *FOX FIRE* AND PEERED into the distance. A sharp speck pierced the line between the plains and the sky. The white spire marked the seat of the Crystalline Queen, and the shadow that sprawled around it would be Lyndon City. On its streets, their two years of sailing the skies as predators would come to an end. In place of the constant windburn and the sharp scent of elemental cannons would be a cage of silks and manners. It all made her coarsened skin itch. Yet *Fox Fire* barreled toward it with as much speed as her groaning liftwood hull could take. At least the air around her seemed to match her mood. The wind whipped at her close-cropped hair and she could taste the coming storm on her tongue. Her broad hand left the comforting sponginess of the bow's railing to clutch at the bandolier she wore across her shoulder. It held many elemental canisters, each as thick as two of her fingers, ammunition for the hand cannon she had holstered at her hip. Her mind flirted with the idea of mixing a fire-and-water canister to throw a cloud of steam in their path and obscure their destination for a few blissful moments.

A laugh, high and mocking, sounded behind Ishe, one she knew very well. Ishe straightened her back and slammed a tight smile on her face before whirling around. Her mother, Madria, grinned at her in a manner that reminded Ishe of the hyena in the Steward's zoo. The crimson red of her admiral's uniform shone even without all the stripes and medals of rank that had been stripped from it. "Staring at the city won't make us arrive any faster, my little Rhino," Madria said, the corner of her lip drawing up into a wicked smirk. "Or slower. No need to invite the kami to intercede when we are so close."

"I am not whispering secret prayers to the wind, Mother," Ishe said, "I would not do that." Desperately, she cataloged everything that she might have done wrong since leaving port, but found no sin that might cause her mother to leave the helm in the middle of a watch.

Madria smiled; this time, it crinkled the crow's feet around her eyes. "Patience." She reached up to take a steadying hold of Ishe's shoulder. "You will have your time to wander the winds without me."

"Yes, Mother," Ishe said by rote as years flashed through her mind. "After Yaki is married, after we've pushed into the trading guilds, after everyone's forgotten that the Shiori are from the hills?" Bitterness crept into her voice.

Madria's smile turned lopsided. "In Lyndon, we will be the Stadbrokes."

Ishe's fists tightened as the frustration began to climb up her spine. "Yesterday, we were going to be the Selbornes!"

That old sly grin crept onto Madria's face again. "That's what I let the dockhands hear. We can't have anyone looking us up from Golden Hills. Did I not wink?"

"No, Mother, you did not." Ishe wondered, not for the first time, what her mother's true family name was. It had been Shiori for years; she had liked that name. A generic Golden Hills House that had died out a hundred years before. Mother's real name probably had more in common with her nickname, Silver Fox, than any proper House. Her broad features were more common among the Low Rivers Tribe than among the nobles of the city. And her name, Madria, that sounded more Lyndonian than anything else. Ishe ached to know the real story of her mother's name, but it remained buried and forgotten under piles of lies like everything else. Crossing her arms, Ishe looked back to the blue expanse of the sky, or rather expected blue expanse, because clouds had appeared on the port side of the ship.

"It does not matter. Listen, girl. For the next few months or years, your sister will need your services." Madria's voice drifted low and serious.

"I fail to see how I'll help her find a sucker to marry other than standing next to her to make her pretty by comparison," Ishe grumbled.

Madria's voice picked up a bit of gravel. "You will have to do that and more, my little Rhino. Family comes first."

Sucking in a bit of cheek, Ishe bit down on it. Family always came first, which meant Mother always came first. "Yes, Mother," Ishe said without conviction.

Hard fingers latched on to Ishe's jaw and pulled her gaze down toward her mother's blazing eyes. "You will need to do *much* better than that! We've sheltered her for a reason, Ishe! However, if the winds blow in another direction, it will be up to you to protect her. From now on, if your sister asks something of you, you will do it. If you see she needs something from your talents, you provide it without being asked. And you will do it all with a smile. Understand?"

Ishe's jaw wobbled from the pain and she had to blink tears out of her eyes. "Yes, M-M-Mum," she managed to stutter, praying it was convincing enough, and mentally slapped herself for not seeing this coming from leagues away. When the skies were calm and change was approaching, her mother's moods became the storm.

Yet the iron grip persisted. Anyone else and Ishe would have sent them sprawling, but she'd never been able to raise so much as a finger against her mother.

Madria eyes drilled into her daughter's as if studying the back of her skull. "You do this for me and I will give you *Fox Fire*."

Ishe's heart stopped. She forgot her jaw. She forgot everything but *Fox Fire*. It had been the first ship captured in the war with Lyndon long before Ishe's birth. and using it, Madria had climbed the ranks from simple sky maiden to the Admiralty. Constructed of priceless southern liftwood, it was the swiftest ship in the fleet in the years of her service. It had been with her mother longer than Ishe could remember; even during the years as a royal consort, it had been her personal pleasure craft. The ship was her mother's feet, its cannons her fists. If she was even thinking of passing it on, it meant she was dead serious about giving up the sky.

And that would make Ishe one of the youngest, if not the youngest, captains in the known blue, even if it took a few years to get the Flower settled. Just a few more years and Ishe would have her freedom. "I'll do it." Ishe spoke the words, trying to shove away the kernel of doubt in her mind. *Please let this be true,* she pleaded with the universe. She'd always assumed that if she ever managed to escape her mother's orbit, she'd have to do it from nothing, but if she had the ship, the possibilities were endless.

Madria patted her cheek affectionately, the iron grip hidden once more within her steady hands. "That's a good girl. Go see your sister."

Nodding, Ishe nearly skipped back toward her sister's cabin.

Ishe did not see her mother's shoulders slump or her hand fall to the sword at her belt. "Hold on to this moment, daughter." Her words were whispered so quietly that only the wind heard them.

Chapter Three

❧

A proper Lady is not an equal to a man; she is far greater.

— MADAM MANA, HEADMISTRESS OF
THE SCHOOL OF THE CULTURED
LADY

YOU ARE TO APPEAR AS A FRESH FLOWER WAITING TO BE plucked. The words of Yaki's tutor sang in her mind as she peered into the mirror. A fist-sized sun crystal illuminated the tiny cabin as if she were in the Steward's garden back home. Powder had lightened her usually reddish terra-cotta complexion to a tawny hue. Would it be enough? The Lyndoners were generally a fairer-skinned folk, but no amount of makeup and dye would turn her shiny black hair white as flax or her deep brown eyes ice blue. Perhaps a beauty crystal could, but the thought of the side effects made her shiver. Instead, she groped for that fine line between acceptable and not being called exotic.

Her mixed heritage spoke on her face; her Golden Hills father had given her wide, nearly feline eyes, which softened Madria's broad northern tribal features. Eyes that could make her look predatory with the right lines or kittenish and innocent with others. Those features would mark her immediately as a foreigner in Lyndon, no matter what her skin tone. She opened the powder box and reached for her brush.

A soft chuckle stopped her. "Stop fretting; you're going to be scooped up and married before you get two feet on the dock."

Yaki smiled and looked at her companion in the small room. The gangly man stooped over a silver teapot, methodically dunking a strainer full of tealeaves. Fifteen dunks, no more, no less. Sparrow never accepted anything but precision when it came to tea. In the simulated sunlight, his pale skin marked him as a Lyndoner or a resident of icy Valhalla far to the south, but when he looked up, if you managed to see past the prominent nose and the mustache that obscured his mouth, the grid of tattooed lines across his eyes and forehead marked him as a member of the Low Rivers Tribe. "I hope for their sake a noble gets to me first; Mother will object otherwise." Yaki smiled her practiced pretty smile, the sort that made most men stammer.

Sparrow glanced up and *tsk*ed as he poured the tea into three earthenware cups. "I give that one a seven. You still look a bit worried."

"There's no reason to worry," she told herself and Sparrow for the thousandth time. "Lyndon's inheritance laws are very generous with young widows." Yaki examined her face and practiced smoothing out the worry lines. Mother wanted a mark, preferably an elderly, doddering man with far more coin than good sense. Yaki's stomach churned as she imagined gnarled hands grasping at her underclothes, their parchment-white skin splattered with liver spots, night after night.

No matter how much she'd been trained, it would be years of endurance, despite everything Mother said. Yaki had learned many things over her eighteen years, and the most painful thing was that the Silver Fox's tongue dripped with empty promises.

The narrow door to the cabin swung open, and the smiling form of Ishe blocked the daylight beyond. The smile was slightly crooked due to a short line of scar tissue, the remnant of a childhood tussle between the twins that had involved a hot poker. Yaki had her own scar from that fight, but it was mercifully below the neckline.

Sparrow thrust out the tray of three cups beneath Ishe's chin before she could speak. "Tea, little miss?" he asked despite the fact that Ishe probably outweighed and outmuscled his spindly frame three to one. Ishe took a cup with a nod of thanks and blew across the tea's surface as Sparrow served Yaki and himself.

The conversation paused as the three imbibed the spicy brew, a concoction of wild yellow herbs that grew on the hills that gave Yaki's home city its name.

Something black and red zipped between Ishe's legs. Yaki squeaked in surprise as Sparrow darted forward, extending a hand into the space between Yaki and the shape. It leaped, expertly spreading its eight fuzzy legs to sail over Sparrow's hand.

"Uff!" Yaki exhaled as the giant spider impacted her stomach.

"Bad Blinky!" Sparrow scolded before shooting a stern look at Ishe. "We were attempting to keep him off the dress. Now we'll be picking spider lint off it until we reach port."

Ishe made a shrug of apology and stepped fully into the room, shutting the door behind her. "He just wants to see it. Didn't he make the threads?"

Blinky, a tame hunting spider that had come with

Sparrow onto *Fox Fire*, had taken no notice of the scolding, instead looking up at Yaki, hopefully searching her face with the largest pair of his eight amber eyes. He stood with seven legs gripping either side of the chair and the last one reaching toward Yaki's free hand. She frowned at the critter. "No… down. Get down."

"*Chrrik! Chrrik!*" The spider shimmied side to side in a playful dance, his eyes blinking a pair at a time. His extended foot claw attempted to guide Yaki's hand back toward his head.

Yaki's frown cracked into a smile after only a second of the spider's antics, and she exhaled with a sigh. Sliding her fingers over his wiry hair, Yaki sunk her long nails into the joint between his head and thorax and scratched at the tough membrane there. Blinky shivered and emitted a series of clicks as he settled into her lap.

"Sorriest excuse for a ship spider ever," Ishe grumbled with a smirk, giving Blinky a quick pet over the red diamond shape on his back. The red crystals in the corners of the shape brightened their glow.

"Did you have something to tell us, sister mine? Does Mother want to tell me how to carry myself for the eyes of the gentlemen? Or was this all a plot to dirty my dress?" Yaki asked, opening an ornately lacquered box that *Fox Fire* had liberated a few months earlier. Inside lay an array of exquisitely crafted pendants, one for each of the Lyndoner saints.

"I'm"—the big girl's round cheeks darkened with the whisper of a blush—"I'm here to offer my help."

"With what?" Yaki's tone climbed skeptically.

"Anything you need. Once we dock, Mother has… ahhhh…informed me that I should do anything you need doing." Ishe knit her fingers and bent them back. Several of them made a sound like two stones clacking together. Yaki shivered as the sound lanced down her spine.

"Ugh, well, for starters, don't do that." Yaki eyed her sister's grin with a growing pit in her stomach. Ishe usually took a command to listen to Yaki about as well as Blinky took to not eating kittens: sourly. Yet from the way Ishe bounced in her spider-skin boots, *enthusiasm* would be too soft a word. "What did Mother promise you?"

"The ship!" Ishe burst out.

Sparrow spewed out a swallow of tea into a fine mist and had a sudden coughing fit.

Ishe barreled on, not even noticing. "Once you're married and settled, I get *Fox Fire*! I'll be the youngest captain the skies have ever seen."

As she had been trained, Yaki inclined her head just so and placed a beatific smile on her lips. "That's wonderful for you," she exclaimed without the slightest indication of sarcasm as her gut roiled. The Rhino would be free on the currents to plunder as her little black heart desired, while Yaki would be locking lips with an incontinent old man who stank of apple brandy. *Because that's fair. Screw Mother, I'm going to marry a young noble instead. Maybe I'll take multiple husbands at once!* Yaki funneled amusement at the thought of a fawning man on each of her arms into her face. Ishe was talking again but Yaki nodded without listening. *I know Lyndoners tend to frown on multiple wives, but do they have a law against multiple husbands? After all, Mistress Tieko said nothing gets the gossip swinging like a good love triangle.*

While Yaki pondered how best to avenge herself on her mother, Ishe stepped around to examine her jewelry box with the four saint pendants. "Trying to decide which one to wear?"

Shaking off her revenge plots, Yaki returned to the present time. "Yes. I…"

Ishe plucked the golden cast of Jules, the Lyndoner saint of industry. The one-inch-tall man clutched a scale in one hand and a wrench in the other. Unlike the others, he was unadorned with gems or polluting metals. Purest gold. "This one. No separate bits for you to swallow."

Yaki allowed herself a sniff of distaste. "I'm not a child."

"You still suck on your jewelry when you're stressed. Mother simply finally trained you out of letting her see it." Ishe smiled triumphantly, as usual mistaking a single witty jab as a victory.

"Dragon HO!" The wooden planks that separated the small cabin from the rest of the deck muffled the booming voice of the lookout, but it was plenty loud enough to penetrate the half-second silence as Yaki constructed her repartee. The insult collided with a stab of terror halfway out her throat. Instantly, both Ishe and Sparrow were rushing for the door heedless of Yaki's sudden coughing fit.

"No. Not now!" Yaki found her voice, but only after she was the only one left in the room.

Chapter Four

Where did the Dragons come from? The Sun Emperor claimed they came from the sea, some tribes point to the sky, others stomp their feet. What is clear? Before the Cataclysm, they weren't here.

— HON NISHAMURA, CHIEF
HISTORIAN OF THE STEWARD'S
ARCHIVES

DRAGON? WHERE? ISHE SPUN ON HER TOES A FEW FEET from Yaki's beauty cabin, her eyes looking up to the crow's nest on the larger of *Fire Fox*'s two masts. Normally, bands of gossamer sails composed of spider silk billowed out from either side to join with the wing masts that extended from the side of the ship, but *Fox Fire* had been under propeller power since they left the Golden Hills. The beautiful sails would only slow them down now. With sails, *Fox Fire* resembled a wind-driven messenger ship, but now there was no disguising the sleek, predatory hull. In the crow's nest, a sailor pointed a red flag aft, the color reserved for dragons and foreign naval vessels.

Sailors were already starting to swarm up from below decks, hurrying to all-hands stations. Ishe gritted her teeth. Mother had already issued orders. Breaking into a run, Ishe thundered across the ship to the rear, nearly bowling over several crewmates. Mother stood on the edge of the poop deck, watching the crew scurry. Behind her, Hawk loomed like a mountain as Ishe pulled herself up the steps.

"Is it true?" were the first words out of Ishe's lips, and she immediately wanted to punch them. The truth of it was written all over Madria's face, in the set of her jaw. Ishe couldn't always tell when her mother was lying, but bad news gave her mother a certain expression.

Madria pointed aft. Ishe followed the finger to see a dark, undulating V against the gray of the clouds they had exited an hour before. Ishe did a quick mental calculation and came to two possibilities. To be that size in front of the clouds meant the lookout had not been paying attention and the V had been flying after them for some time. Or that dragon was as big as *Fox Fire*.

"Mother, that's—"

"A very large duck that needs to be shot out of the sky. Ishe, you take the portside battery, and Hawk will supervise the starboard. We will execute a drop roll as he closes. We will have one opportunity to damage the dragon's wings. Understood?" Madria said in her captain's voice.

"Yes, Captain." Ishe saluted. Hawk merely nodded.

"Go on, Hawk. Ishe, stay a moment," Madria said. The big woman vaulted the railing down to the main deck and landed with barely a sound.

Ishe pulled her hand down to her side. "Yes, Mother?"

Madria's eyes remained hard. "Ishe, if the first volley misses, *Fox Fire* is likely to be lost."

Ishe swallowed, momentarily confused. Did her mother somehow doubt her after two years of sailing? "I won't miss, Mother. I won't let a single scale touch *Fox Fire*. She's mine, too."

Her mother shook her head and sighed sadly. "Are you captaining now, Ishe?"

"Uh...no, Ma—ma'am."

"Then you don't go down with the ship. As soon as you fire the shot after the drop roll, I want you moving toward the gliders." Madria's voice softened. For the first time, Ishe noticed the deep bags under her eyes and took a step back, not wanting to see the hopelessness there. Madria doublestepped to close the gap. "The crew and I will make one more attempt if we can while you and Yaki get a head start. The crew will follow; he'll probably want to parley."

"M-M-Mother?!" Defeat was already written on Madria face as if the battle had happened while Ishe wasn't looking. That couldn't be possible. The Silver Fox had never been beaten in the sky. Her name was whispered in quiet awe amongst the taverns and pubs in every port Ishe had been to. Ishe reached down inside, found her spine, and tried again. "Mother, I'm third-in-command. You can't treat me like—"

A knife appeared in Madria's hand as if by magic, although Ishe knew it had been put there via a spring-loaded mechanism hidden in the sleeve. That knowledge did not change the fact that this particular knife did not usually appear without being embedded in someone. Ishe shut up.

"You have a choice, my little Rhino. You can obey your mother or go to the infirmary right now." Madria's voice became shimmering steel as she pressed the flat of the blade against Ishe's chest.

An old scar on her forearm twinged as Ishe looked away.

"I'll take that dragon down with one shot, Mother," Ishe said through gritted teeth.

"Good shot or no, you make sure your back is to that cannon after the shot. Understand?"

Ishe nodded. The knife disappeared and Madria's hand was patting her cheek affectionately. "Good girl. Hop to it."

Turning without another word, Ishe lurched for the stairs with her ears burning. Her mother would always be the one wall she'd never be able to charge through.

Fortunately, there was a simple solution to this: put so many holes in that dragon's wings as to convert the flying reptile into a falling one. Ishe grinned as she stalked to the portside battery. She liked simple solutions.

The gunners were already in place at the eight elemental cannons that made up the portside battery. Not all the cannons were equal. In the middle lay two monstrous weapons, steelwood trunks reinforced with brass and studded with green shock-absorbing crystals. These had been constructed to hurl huge Earth crystal charges, the sort that opened up holes in steel-plated warships. Provided the gems held and nothing exploded, they'd throw a charge nearly a mile if fully powered.

The gunner of the largest cannon, Koshue, was already at his post, checking the chains that prevented the thing from launching across the deck. Bald as a bean, he wore his long-braided beard tossed over his shoulder to keep it out of the way. That's how you knew he was a good gunner. The man hadn't singed his beard in over a decade.

"Koshue, you said you could convert this cannon to an elemental lance." Ishe looked back toward the aft of the ship. The bow had tilted upward as *Fox Fire* climbed higher, revealing the flapping V of the dragon. "You have about fifteen minutes."

The man didn't even flinch. "I need a direct line to the

power crystal for that," Koshue said, already pulling his toolbox from his gunner's pit behind the cannon.

"You'll have it." Ishe raised her voice to include the rest of the battery, "Cannons one, two, seven, and eight, load long-range-fire charges! Three, five, and Six, prep Earth shot. Once loaded, prep for drop maneuvers. Go!"

Gunners exploded into motion. The smaller cannons on the edges of the battery had already been loaded, so their crews began to place poles into the slots in the deck where they locked in with a click. These poles had metal rings running up their length that the gunners could clip their harnesses to and not go flying during maneuvers. The large central cannons had to be unloaded and then reloaded with cluster ammunition. Ishe flagged down a runner and dispatched a message to engineering. Then the waiting period began as the V of the dragon grew.

Ishe pulled a small spyglass from her belt and pointed it at the oncoming beast. Within the glass, the V took on malicious details. The heavy, bulky body bobbled between the wings, and huge antlers curled back from the dragon's head. Ishe's heart fell out of her chest and attempted to hide in her intestines. The antlers, like those of the world's most glorious stag, marked their pursuer as one very specific dragon. One dragon who was three hundred years dead: the scourge of the Golden Hills, Yaz'noth, the Horned Serpent. Three hundred years before, he had reduced half the city to ash and would have finished the job had the navy not managed to separate his head from his body. It hung in the great hall where Ishe had dined for years: cold and still, but giving the impression it might come alive at any moment.

Now he had. Ishe swallowed and watched as Yaz'noth, who had taken on an entire navy, flew free from the grave and directly at *Fox Fire*.

Chapter Five

Liftwood is not a gift of the gods, but the aftermath of draconic laziness. During the height of the Empire of the Grand Wyrm, tired of burning the roads between cities, a dragon named Grac'sar cultivated a plant that allowed his servants to take to the skies. He disappears from the record shortly afterward.

> — HON NISHAMURA, CHIEF
> HISTORIAN OF THE STEWARD'S
> ARCHIVES

PLINK-PLINK. YAKI'S EARRINGS LANDED IN THE TIN CUP. Several rings followed as she peeled them from her long fingers.

"Yaki! Get your dolly-dinkled tushy in here!" a voice screeched from the other side of the thick metal door she stood in front of.

"I'm coming, you hairy spitwad!" Yaki shouted back,

yanking off the last ring, which claimed a small piece of her finger's skin as a trophy. She looked down at her finely pleated skirts and swore. It had to be her best dress, her very best dress, of course. Sparrow would surely strangle her if they survived this dragon. Still, muscle memory overcame her reluctance; she grabbed a foot-long rod with a razor-sharp hook fastened to one end. With a practiced motion, she swung it back behind her and, with an upward tug, sliced through all the strings that secured her bodice. The dress didn't want to let her go so easily. The skintight velvet sleeves had to be peeled off her arms before the rest of it slipped down onto the greasy floor. Yaki kicked it into a larger tin bin before throwing herself at the wall of safety gear.

"What you doing in there? Ya makeup?" the voice came again as Yaki slid into a pair of buffalo-hide overalls. She ignored him as she followed the overalls up with a leather jacket reinforced with chain, gloves that reached her elbows, and a helmet with a clear faceplate that was stronger than any mere glass.

Thus clad from head to her ankles with only her feet bare, Yaki swung the door open to *Fox Fire*'s engine room. A rush of air made the frayed bits of Yaki's armor dance as her nose filled with the electric scent of magic. She strode in, head tilted up at the figure hanging from the chains that crisscrossed the ceiling. "About time you got here. Julia is getting real cross. We need to calm her down before things get heavy," said Murray, the ship's mechanic, hanging upside down by means of a thick, furry tail that protruded from the seat of his overalls. Other than the overalls, the old man wore no protection. Although the various scars, burns, and cuts that pockmarked his simian-like features illustrated perfectly why Mother had insisted on the helmet. His face, with a broad nose and deep-set eyes that burned with a cutting intellect, was the most human thing about Murray. The rest of him appeared to be a fight between a monkey and a gorilla with a dash of grumpy old man for flavoring.

"Aye aye." Yaki nodded, grabbing the chain to her left and scurrying up into the overhead web with practiced ease, bare toes gripping. She started moving for the dominant feature in the engine room, the huge, glowing crystal that pulsed with electric blue light overwhelming the glow crystals embedded in the ceiling. This was Julia, a power crystal twelve feet long and six feet wide at the middle, the heart of *Fox Fire*. The bulky machinery that crowded at the floor had one purpose: to convert Julia's energy into motion, hence, keeping the *Fox Fire* afloat in the sky. The ship was small to have such a large crystal. To handle that much power, most ships required an engine room twice the size. But Murray had solved that problem by simply leaving no room to walk between the various converters, switches, and shunts. Instead, if you needed to fix something, you hung upside down from the chains. It wasn't easy and it took longer, but it worked and that's what counted. It was a configuration that would only be thought of by a crystal-touched engineer.

Becoming touched was an occupational hazard for any who worked with high-quality crystals. Touching a crystal as it overloaded or exploded could warp the mind and body. Murray's origins were more exotic: the Lyndon trading vessel he crewed crashed into the very edge of a forest composed entirely of crystal somewhere in the north. Reality within those borders swam like a fish. Most of the crew didn't survive the mile's walk out. Yaki had made the mistake of asking about that walk once, and what Murray had told her still seeded her nightmares with images of people being turned inside out.

Yaki made it to the center and, lacking a tail, hung upside down over the crystal via a support line attached to her belt. She reached out toward the crystal, gloved fingers spread. Closing her eyes, she concentrated on feeling the warmth pulsing through her fingers. She had always thought of it as a heartbeat. The crystal's vibrations fluttered through her veins and entangled themselves with her own pulse, which accelerated to match. Yaki took a deep breath and thought of a brilliant blue sky. She thought of *Fox Fire* sailing through it, unconcerned. No predators. No prizes to take. *Just sky,* she thought to the crystal. *Just sky.*

A churning whirl of discontent pushed back, triggering memories of aching backs and sore legs that Yaki had gathered from her short lifetime of dance and fencing practice. Julia, like everything else in the world, had its own kami. Growing up, Yaki had served as a shrine maiden to Grandmother Willow, one of the few trees in the city that remembered the great burning. Yaki had learned to listen to the elderly tree's whispers. Julia, by comparison, shouted through the ship like an angry drunk demanding another bottle of beer. She adored the twisted engineer with a deep longing, and bitterly resented the rest of the machinery for taking his attention away from her.

Yaki sent back sympathetic thoughts: the ghost of a smile she got from Mother when she performed a dance or song, the pleasure of applause, assuring the spirit within that all the hard work was worth it and that the crew appreciated what she had done.

The pulse of the crystal slowed. *Good girl,* Yaki thought at it, thanking it. A year and a half earlier, Yaki had been sent to the engine room as a punishment. She no longer remembered why. But once Murray had noticed that Yaki could calm Julia, it had become her permanent station despite the constant risk machinery posed to her marketability. Fortunately, years of dance training had rendered her nimble enough to avoid major harm so far.

Opening her eyes, Yaki looked around. Murray worked

on the impellers that drove one of the drive shafts. Thick shafts of ironwood pierced either side of the engine room. Cut from a single massive tree, each shaft stretched all the way out of the ship's stern, where they were tipped with the propellers. sixteen blocks of high-capacity liftwood ringed the driveshaft at regular intervals. By shocking the blocks one at a time with a power nozzle, the upward motion turned the shaft. Two days of constant use of the impellers had taken its toll, and the rings were scorched with black. Nothing could be done about that unless they stopped the shaft's spin. Instead, Murray busied himself cleaning the impellers so the power would arc cleanly. Normally, Yaki would have been down there doing the same for her shift, but she had been on beauty rest until this point. The two young engine hands, Jack and Jill, worked the other driveshaft.

Sensing her eyes on him, Murray looked up with a leer. "You calm my grumpy old bitch down, Prissy Missy?"

Yaki nodded. "She's all calm, chief."

"Good; fetch us the spare rings. Your mum's goanna execute a turn soon. Then we'll see who's fastest at replacing a ring." Murray said.

"Aye." Yaki turned before Murray could see her scowl as Jack and Jill tittered. Her stomach always twisted at these farcical contests, Murray's attempt to massage Jack and Jill's egos after Yaki communed with the crystal. It was something the two ex-stowaways from Valhalla might never learn to do. Yaki was no stranger to losing, but losing on purpose left a bitter aftertaste. Swinging over to the supply closet, Yaki grabbed three spare rings, a hammer, and several bags of nails. "Which side?" she asked.

"Turning to port, then depending on the beastie after us, we might snake around to starboard or do a drop-and-roll to get a shot at its belly," Murry said. Yaki instinctually jiggled her wrists up and down, feeling the weight of the heavy bracelet she always wore on her left wrist, reminding herself which direction was port and which was starboard. "If we replace these rings, we might get enough speed to escape without getting more than our tails singed."

Yaki distributed the rings, hurling the one at Jack and Jill slightly harder than necessary.

The door to the engine room burst open. A crewman, a year younger than Yaki, stumbled through the door, nearly falling into the equipment. "We need a line to the power core!"

Murray's head snapped toward him with a feral grimace. "What? Says who, boy?"

The boy gave a quick explanation of Ishe's conversion of one of the cannons into an elemental lance.

"Queen's a-crackin'!" Murray swore, and jabbed a hairy finger at Jill. "Run the damn line, Jill. Tell Ishe that if she fires that blighted thing at any point other than the drop, I'll use her skull as an oil filter." He shifted his gaze to Yaki, who had made no attempt to hide her smirk. "And don't you ask me how that'd work, Priss! I'd figure it out. Jill, get a-moving. Everyone else: positions now!"

Jill scrambled up the lines, her skinny form handling the chains as if she'd been born on them. She swung back to Julia's base and plugged in one of the emergency cables. In order for the liftwood that composed the hull of the ship to provide lift and not be dead weight, it had to be connected to Julia. The inside of the hull was a web work of wiring. The system didn't have much redundancy, so a lucky shot could depower a swath of hull. To make up for this, Murray had threaded emergency cables throughout the ship that could be easily rerouted to depowered areas. Yaki had never figured out which cable went where, as Mother's orders were to stay in the armored engine room for all battles.

As Jill and the runner exited, Yaki moved so she hung

upside down over one of the three impeller rings on the port-side drive shaft, hammer with its clawed side posed to strike. The replacement ring, in four sections, hung in a sleeve on its own chain two feet away but in easy reach. Jack had an identical setup on the other side of the room. Murray, in the middle, hung on to the chains above with his tail, the sections of ring grasped in his long, finger-like toes. All three pairs of eyes watched the gauge that was connected to levers placed on the poop deck, like horses waiting for the swing of a green flag.

"Don't have to be pretty. It's just gotta work," Murray growled before lapsing into silence. Yaki listened to her heartbeat away the time. Ishe wanted to use an elemental lance, the naval equivalent of a shiv. If Mother had allowed it, then this wouldn't be one of the younger dragons, hungry for metals. The hull was loaded with only gold, silver, and a chest of gems. The majority of it was intended for her dowry, the rest to be divided among the crew. The spoils of two years of piracy, and more than half of it pulled from a motherlode of a quicksilver shipment last week. Could that massively expensive shipment be connected?

The gauge for the port propeller throttle swung from cruise to full stop. As one, the three of them pulled the arc emitters away from the impeller rings. Even as the heavy shaft still spun, Yaki swung her hammer down into the side of the scorched wood, hoping to use the log's momentum to pry the old ring off.

Chapter Six

"The ancients did not need liftwood to fly; they propelled metal into the sky and beyond with nothing but fire. No torchship can do that."

— HON NISHAMURA, CHIEF
HISTORIAN OF THE STEWARD'S
ARCHIVES

ISHE SUCKED IN THE RAPIDLY THINNING AIR AS THE SHIP slowly began to swing around to bring her cannon to bear on the Horned Dragon. All the men were strapped in. Ishe herself stood between two wooden posts ten feet back from the line of cannon. Two straps from her belt to the posts secured her to the posts. Koshue and his assistants had reworked the mount so the newly refitted lance could be swung. "Long-range cannons on my mark! Aim!" Ishe commanded as the gunners manning the four smallest cannons tensed. "Left side will fire, call out coordinates, and fire. Right side will adjust aim and then fire."

A murmur of *aye*s met her instructions and the human sound died away; the entire ship momentarily quiet, the only sounds the gentle *whup whup whup* of the propellers and the groaning of the liftwood as it fought to rise higher. They had the high sky for now, but the crew would be reaching their limit soon. Slowly, the beating wings of the dragon moved into the firing arc.

"Fire one!" Ishe called. Two cannons barked their answer, their gunners calling out their markings. Two shells, glowing like flung embers, arced through the sky and came up far short. Ishe revised her estimate of the dragon's size yet again.

"Adjusting," the right cannoneer called out. "Ready."

"Fire!" Ishe called.

These twin shells arced out true. The dragon swerved slightly to avoid the charges, which exploded harmlessly below him. He glided for a moment and executed a slight waggle with his wings, waving hello.

Three shapes leapt from his back as they spread their own wings. Ishe's jaw fell. Shock and murmurs of despair rippled among the gunners. Four dragons.

Four dragons against one lone, small sloop of a ship. Even a great steel-sided *Behemoth* would be quaking against four dragons of any size. Dragons were not pack animals and they did not hunt together. There were no records of dragons working together since the fall of the Great Wyrm's Empire. And yet there they were. Four dragons, the three smaller ones rapidly climbing, while their granddaddy kept barreling toward the ship.

My ship, Ishe reminded herself. *Fox Fire* would be hers, and no dragons, no matter how big or how many, were going to take it from her without a fight. "Reload!" she bellowed.

"Cannons three, four, and six, change shot for Fire shells. Don't let those whelpings get above us!"

The gunners did a collective double take at her.

"You going to die on your feet or on your asses?" Ishe yelled with a fury. "Hop to!"

The gunners dived into their tasks. Ishe looked back over the deck; men were scurrying up the masts, rigging up a large triangular sail that would greatly improve *Fox Fire*'s turning. With that deployed, Mother could waggle the ship to bring the other side into firing position while Ishe's battery reloaded, but it would cost them accuracy. She turned back to the portside battery with a huff and watched one sailor struggle to secure the breech of the cannon. "All ready?" she called. The loading crews raised their fists in reply as the gunners aimed, adjusting the dials of each cannon.

"Fire!" The cannon sounded and a line of seven embers was belched out into the sky, arcing toward the cluster of smaller dragons. Their wings stopped pumping as all three fell into a brief dive to avoid the shells. Ishe's lips curled back from her teeth. The cannon took too long to load and fire for the volleys to be effective. "Fire down the line. Koshue, fire at will!"

"Aye!" the crew called back. The cannoneers began to load and fire as fast as they could. Shots began to ring out every three to five seconds as they staggered. A single shell cost the dragons nearly as much time as a volley. It was working.

Then the three dragons split off from each other. Two still climbed, in opposite directions, while the third leveled off, sailing on a trajectory that would put him beneath *Fox Fire*. But the closer the dragon got, the less time he'd have to dodge. Ishe grinned.

"Koshue!" she called. "Knock that bottom dragon out of the sky!"

"Aye, m'lady." The gunner wheezed and sighted on the dragon through his targeting grid. He began to call out adjustments, which were quickly carried down the line. Ishe squeezed down on her supports, wishing not for the first time she knew the guns even half as well as Koshue. Her stomach whirled as the guns were nudged without her input or judgment. Ishe cringed, waiting for Mother to materialize at her left shoulder and ask her questions.

"Mark!" Koshue called out, raising his fist and stopping Ishe from nervously looking over her shoulder. The other gunners quickly followed suit.

"Fire!" Ishe called, and the guns answered, firing in sequence from outer to the inner. Three shots in a triangle dove in front of the dragon and exploded into three points of death. The dragon was forced to swerve around, only to be driven back by the second salvo. Koshue had constructed a ring of death with the last shot, the shell forming a circle with a shining shell of steely blue in the middle, an ice shell. Among the ember-red shells and their dazzling explosions, the dragon didn't even attempt to dodge the last shell. It exploded in a blast of electric blue-green. The dragon, coated in the shine of ice in sunlight, fell toward the ground like a stone.

A cheer went up, Ishe's own voice included before she remembered herself and shouted, "Reload!" She didn't have time to wonder what orifice Koshue had pulled that ice shell from.

But the focus had cost them. The remaining two dragons had climbed out of the cannon's firing arcs, wings pumping like sparrows being chased by hawks.

The dead drop would be next. They'd have to use it to avoid one of the smaller dragons' strike. "Load shot!" Ishe called.

The whispers around her grew to a howl as a fresh wind slammed across the bow of the ship.

———

YAKI BLINKED STINGING SWEAT FROM HER EYES AS SHE clambered into the web work of chains to admire their handiwork. All the impeller rings had been replaced, and both propeller shafts were spinning too fast for any details of the wood to be seen. The power arcing from the emitters to the impellers was just short enough to be tolerated; there had been no time to align anything. The apparatus was spinning. That was the important thing. And they would carry *Fox Fire* faster than any dragon could fly.

"Hah. Not bad, Prissy Missy." Murray's huge hand swatted her on the back, sending her swinging. "That's the way!" he whooped as the airspeed gauge slowly ticked upward toward an eye-watering twenty knots.

The hull groaned and the gauge redlined. Ishe's jubilant heart dived down into her toes. Murray swung back to his engineering nest over Julia's midsection; he lifted the horn of the intercom to his ear and stuck an oversize digit in his other. Yaki shared anxious glances with Jack and Jill as Murray's head began to nod at the unheard commands from Captain Madria. Murray's eyes strayed to Yaki for a brief moment, and she knew she'd been singled out for something.

Yaki forced herself to smile back, and the monkey man turned away with a grimace. Poker-faced, Murray was not.

He slammed the horn back into its cradle with more force than necessary. Yellow teeth were bared at it in an inhuman expression of malice. "A headwind has come out of nowhere. It's blowing us backward." He pointed at the maxed-out gauge. "The dragons are climbing above us. We're to prepare for a half-dead swing. Jack and Jill, man the cabling. Yaki, prep the shield crystal. I want to use every ounce of power Julia can give us. Waste nothing."

"Aye." Yaki echoed somewhat belatedly, her mind reeling from the word *dragons*. Not one, but at least two. Her mind filled with all manner of ideas about that word as she climbed into the chain webbing and hurried toward what she'd always thought of as the back of the engine room. It was the farthest spot from the door, behind Murray's nest. Along that wall stood *Fox Fire*'s last-ditch defense, a perfectly spherical crystal. Inside it, a storm raged in a whirl of jagged objects. Originally intended for a Valhalla battle cruiser, it took nearly all the power Julia had on offer to use. Ishe looked back to see Murray suspended from his nest, hands spread wide an inch from Julia's surface. His lips moved as he communed with the crystal, and her hum grew to fill the engine room. The drive shafts began to squeal as they spun, the new rings beginning to fill the room with a haze of smoke as *Fox Fire* struggled to beat the wind.

THE WIND WHIPPING AT ISHE'S HAIR SMELLED SOUR, like the air it carried had curdled. She had never mastered the wind's language like Mother, but she could always sniff out bad medicine, and this freak headwind was full of it. With the ship practically frozen in place, Madria had *Fox Fire* diving and rising, searching for friendlier wind.. No new orders had come, leaving Ishe to chew her cheeks and watch as the pair of dragons climbed into an overhead position.

A screech of protesting metal attracted her attention to the starboard battery. Apparently, Hawk had tired of watching the dragons climb into position as well. She had hoisted an entire cannon out of its mount, snapping the steel chains that secured it with her bare hands. It was one of the smaller cannons, but it still reached the giant woman's bosom as she stood it on the deck. She heaved, lifting the cannon and putting it back into the reinforced mount, but backward and pointing straight up. "Fill the air with shot!" she bellowed. Around her, her crew raced to grab whatever personal shell thrower they possessed. Ishe cursed herself for not thinking of it as well.

Ishe slammed one of her two spread-shot shells into her hand cannon. "Aim them up if you got them!" Ishe sighted on the two dragons high above. They looked like oddly shaped eagles at this distance, their wings pumping against the thin air.

"Fire!" Hawk cried, and the starboard threw up a hail of shot. The smaller hand cannons fell short, but Hawk's ship cannon caught the edge of a dragon's wing mid-pump. It shuddered in the air for a moment, wings no longer able to propel it upward, before gliding into a circle. Ishe's breath caught as the sunlight sparkled off its eyes, which peered down at them.

"It's gonna drop!" someone shouted.

"Secure all hands!" Madria's command screamed out as the dragon snapped its wings to its body and began to fall. While a dragon's breath was a fearsome thing against lift-wood hulls, their true weapon lay in the fact they were as dense as the metal that armored their bodies. If the dragons managed to knock out the cables that powered the liftwood, the ship would fall from the sky as well.

Ishe grabbed hold of her supports as the entire deck swung away from her feet. The half-dead drop. The shrill whistle of the falling dragon grew, but Ishe couldn't help watching as the starboard railing plunged below the horizon and revealed the shining golden prairie far below. A single ammo create that some knucklehead had forgotten to secure first sliding and then tumbling over the railing. The whistle grew to a scream as the black shape of the dragon fell past the ship, its entire body tucked into a lethal ball. It hit nothing, not even a mast.

"Orders, Lieutenant?" Koshue rasped.

With a mental curse, Ishe tore her eyes off the falling dragon. With the entire ship vertical, her guns were pointed directly up! "Fire!" Ishe coughed, wrenching herself around to look upward. "Fire at will!"

The guns exploded in a spray of fire, seeking to puncture the last dragon's wings. Yet it had curled into a ball, hiding its head under its tail, and begun to fall, passing through the storm of detonating fire without a wobble. This dragon's aim was true. Pressing her lips together, she managed to muffle her own scream of frustration. *If only she'd loaded the cannons with shot instead of watching Hawk.* "Man the elemental lance!" she nearly screeched. But the ship groaned as the starboard side liftwood came back to life and the ship began to right herself.

There would be no window to use her secret weapon.

Chapter Seven

❦

Crystal-powered weapons delivered humanity from the dragons nearly a thousand years ago. In those days, they were rare things, handed down from wielder to wielder.

— HON NISHAMURA, CHIEF
HISTORIAN OF THE STEWARD'S
ARCHIVES

"SHOWTIME, PRISSY MISSY!" MURRAY'S MAD CACKLE CUT through the din of the engine room. Julia's hum had deepened into a near-subsonic cry of pain; the intensity of it reached into Yaki's skull and pulsed through her chest. The crystal was pouring everything it had into the drive shafts, trying to vainly to beat the wind that had them in its grip. Murray had been forced to choke back the current or the entire drive shaft would burst into flame. That left one trick, the shield crystal, and that was Yaki's job.

Yaki ripped off her gloves and placed her hands on the

crystal's smooth surface. Lightning from the crystal's internal storm licked at her fingertips.

Eager. Gimme gimme gimme. the shield crystal babbled in her mind, hungry for Julia's current.

"I'm ready." Yaki nodded at Murray and he flipped the switch that shunted nearly all of the power Julia produced to the shield crystal, keeping just enough to stay afloat. The great drive staffs went silent. The shield crystal emitted a high-pitched song of electric joy. The storm within it spun and grew as power built. As Yaki concentrated, the storm called out to her, pulled at her. The lightning reached beyond the limits of the crystal to encircle her fingers, then hands, and with a sudden yank, she was launching head first into the storm. Opening like a great eye, the crystal's energy swallowed her and blackness closed around her.

Light. A single point of it blossomed in the distance. Distantly downward. Yaki fell. The point grew, resolved first into a line, then a shape. Details were added like a memory being summoned from the murky depths of a mind: the curve of her hull, the rigid shape of the masts and the barrels of the cannons. Darkness was falling toward the light; its details were also added as she drew closer. A bulbous, ugly thing of heavy metal, a dragon. This was the thing that she must stop.

In the crystal space, everything moved as if the world had become a flipbook. Just a flipbook: after you flipped it, the page disappeared. Here, Yaki was *Fox Fire* and she could see everything *Fox Fire* could. The current flowed into her hands, and it grew brilliant as pages of time ticked away. The current contained everything Julia had. The propellers stopped and the liftwood hull had gone silent. In a moment, the ship would begin to fall. Fortunately, Yaki only needed a moment. She reached out toward the dragon and poured her power into the air.

Bricks and mortar surged into existence before her. A stout wall as wide as the dragon itself assembled in midair. In the real world, she knew crackling green energy would be manifesting where she built her wall, but here, it always felt more solid and real. With the mortar assembled, she reinforced the wall with bands of steel until she had no more power to build. Barring anything else, she placed her ethereal hands behind the wall and braced for the impact. She let time go flipping onward.

The shield crystal had been taken from a military supply ship that had been blown off course by a storm. It was masterwork of crystalline engineering far beyond the ken of the Golden Hills; ships equipped with enough power crystals could endure entire broadsides without a scratch. One Lyndon ship possessed two. It had been christened *Invincible*. Yet a dragon, weighing several tons and falling at terminal velocity, was not a hollow shell filled with unstable crystal fragments.

In the world of the shield crystal, the dragon made no sound as it hit the barrier. Her wall buckled her supports and reinforcements snapping like cheap twine. The arms she had braced against it broke like dry twigs, sending pain lancing through Yaki's mind, ethereal or not. The dragon bounced upward a few feet before crashing onto the deck, inches short of the railing. The cannoneers went scrambling for cover as the wall exploded into a shower of debris.

Searing white filled her vision as something yanked her hard from behind.

"Did it work?" Murray's voice pierced through the light. "How much damage?"

Yaki blinked to clear her eyes and her arms felt alive with electric worms. "None so far. It landed on the deck. I think it's stunned," she gasped. Murray's arm was wrapped around her and held her so tightly, her breath came up short.

A fearsome roar shook the ship and they swayed. "Not stunned enough!" Murray kicked his feet out and hoisted them upward, wrapping his toes around the chain. With effortless ease, he swung them across the engine room, flipping from foot to free hand to foot again before dismounting in front of the engine room's door. They were out the door before Yaki could even voice a protest.

Murray did not pause as he threw the door open and sprinted as fast as his bowed legs would carry him through the antechamber and out into the cargo hold. They passed alongside all the exposed wires that buzzed with the current they transferred to the liftwood hull. Each plank, nearly a foot thick, had to be rigged separately to the power source to ensure proper lift.

"Murray, stop." Yaki finally found her voice as she realized where Murray was rushing. "It's not that bad!" The sharp sound of splitting timber echoed her phrase. Murray continued to carry her as if she weighed nothing at all. "Murray, please!" she pleaded, and began to kick. "I don't have my gear! I need boots! I'm barefoot!" She tried to struggle, but Murray had her arms pinned to her sides.

"Following orders," he grunted. "First the Flower, then the Rhino. Glad I just have to haul your scrawny ass overboard. Hope the captain's got a whole crew assigned to handle your sister." They arrived at the starboard bow. Set into it was a hatch, a circle of wood three feet wide in the hull of *Fox Fire*. Neatly stacked around it were folded gliders, one for each of the crew. Murray set Yaki down and pointed to a small chest by the hatch. "Extra pair of boots in there, along with your rapier. Take one of the sacks of gems; the other is for your sister. If *Fox Fire* goes down, make your way to Lyndon. Go to Butterworth's and ask to speak to the papersmith. Captain says she loves you." Murray's voice cracked a little bit on that last sentence.

Yaki turned and stared at him, mouth agape. This couldn't be happening. They'd been in some close scrapes over the last two years, , but Mama had always had an extra trick up her sleeve. Always managed to come out on top. Hell, the Valhallan Navy had even boarded them once, and this plan had not kicked in.

"Stop staring and get going, you prissy git! We've got a grand wyrm on our tail! The faster you git, the faster I can get back to Jack and Jill." He made a shooing gesture and wiped the back of his broad nose with his hand.

Yaki gave a weak nod and threw herself into the well-practiced evacuation drill, trying to ignore the blurring of her vision and listening to the din of combat above.

Chapter Eight

❧✿❧

Dragons are flying rocks. They shouldn't fly yet, they do.
At least they have the decency to require wings.

— SHINTO YASAMOTO, AUTHOR OF
DRAGON HUNTING WITHOUT DYING

THE RHINO STUFFED ANOTHER SHELL DOWN INTO THE
breech of her hand cannon. Muscle memory snapped it
closed and brought the weapon level with her eyes. Blue
flared from the muzzle of the gun as the shell arced towards
the dragon's head. Its scales shone like a pile of newly minted
pennies, but the only color that reached Ishe's mind was the
bloody red of rage.

The shell struck true, sending ice rushing over the head
and onto its long neck. Cool air swept over the deck of *Fox
Fire* as the blue glow faded, leaving the dragon's head and
neck encased in a half a foot of crystalline ice. Yaki pulled
another shell from her bandolier, not looking at the contents

and not caring. The thing's hooked claws bit into the deck as it continued to pull its heavy body up over the side.

"No NO! *NO!*" Ishe screamed and fired again. *Fox Fire* was hers! All hers! And this beast would not take it away! The force of a tornado howled out from the barrel, sending a deck full of debris whirling toward the dragon. The thick ice shattered as the dragon caught a piece of the railing with its head.

Click. Slam. Aim. Fire. The shell burned a red trail of smoke behind it as it whizzed over the dragon's shoulder. Ishe distantly heard the faint scream of her own frustration and other sounds. She ignored it. There was nothing but *Click. Slam.* Aim. Fire. A blue shell hit the monster in the chest this time. Ice crawled across the scaly skin, down its front legs, and further adhered the dragon to the deck. At least it wouldn't be able to dodge.

Click. Slam. Aim. Fire. A yellow shell struck the front of the thing. Thunder staggered Ishe backward as the dragon's body lifted clear from the deck, claws ripping up planks as it fought to hold on. The dragon's huge head snapped forward, biting into an exposed beam, preventing its fall off the ship. A feral grin of victory spread across Ishe's face. One more shell. She looked down at herself long enough to pull her sole remaining concussion shell from her bandolier. Her hand flew through the ordered sequence.

Click. Slam. Aim. Fire.

Nothing happened. Ishe blinked and realize there was a very large finger interposed between the weapon's hammer and the firing pin. The finger led to a huge hand, which led to a huge arm, which was attached to a very angry-looking Hawk.

Ishe barely had time to register this before an open-handed blow caught her across her jaw. She pinwheeled, the deck slapping against her palms as she fell to her knees.

"Listen to your mother, girl." Hawk delivered the words in a harsh whisper thick with disapproval.

Confusion flavored with hurt fizzed up into Ishe's mind. What had she done wrong? The dragon had to be expelled or the ship would be lost. And she had almost had it! One more shell, just one more.

"Hawk, take her below, strap her to a glider, and throw her overboard."

Ishe looked up into her mother's cold eyes and instantly knew her sin. Her mind helpfully replayed all the voices she had ignored her rage. Particularly the "Ishe! Cease fire!" part. Terror and shame tried to crawl up her throat as Hawk grabbed her arm, lifted her clear from the deck, and dropped her onto her feet.

"But what about the dragon?" Ishe screamed. The beast was clawing his way back onto the ship. One breath of fire and the entire deck would go up like a pile of dry kindling.

"That is not the one you need to be worried about." Hawk jerked her arm and Ishe faced aft. Again, a bolt of understanding crashed through her mind. The great horned dragon had closed the gap, his wings pumping as he surged toward *Fox Fire*. They had minutes before he caught them.

From the corner of her eye, Ishe watched her mother pull a curved katana from a sheath at her side. The crystals that lined the blade began to arc power between them; the pitch of the wind changed from defiant to fearful. This sword was Wind Slicer. Madria settled into a fighting stance and advanced on the dragon. "Go, Hawk," she said without looking back, "take her below. May winds guard your souls and Coyote amuse himself with our enemies."

"Aye, Captain," Hawk said, as she drove Ishe down into the darkened hold. Ishe missed the ladder and tumbled down. Hawk jumped down after her. There was no struggle as Hawk marched her through the bowels of the ship, her steely fingers clamped on Ishe's neck. Rhinos are made of bone and Hawk was pure tempered steel. Ishe tried to bargain instead. "What is she planning to do?"

Hawk didn't respond to the question, just kept pushing her.

"Come on, Hawk. Give me something. What's the plan?"

The question was not met by anything other than more force toward the bow and increasing pressure on her neck. Only after Ishe was shoved toward the gliders and escape hatch did Hawk speak: "Survive. That is the plan. You and your sister are to survive."

Ishe shrugged into the glider, tightened the harness. "What about you and Sparrow and the rest of the crew?"

"Women and children first. The crew will follow," Hawk said as she grabbed Ishe's harness and pulled her to the hatch.

"I'm not—" was all Ishe got out before Hawk threw her into the sky.

Chapter Nine

The Steward's power over paper, a gift given by the Sun-wrought Emperor, strikes me as tad quixotic, as sunlight is no friend to my books.

— HON NISHAMURA, CHIEF
HISTORIAN OF THE STEWARD'S
ARCHIVES

YAKI BIT BACK A SCREAM, IF ONLY TO AVOID GIVING HER heart an escape route. Instead, it thundered in her chest and ears, even louder than air rushing past them. The golden grass of the lowlands stretched out below her, rippling like the hide of a great beast. *If only I were a flea,* Yaki thought, *fleas do not go* splat *when they land on a dog.* Reaching up, her rapidly numbing fingers found the handles and jerked. The paper wings of the glider unfolded with a whoosh, the straps slamming up against her chest. Her legs snapped downward, pain flaring in her hips as gravity tried to rip them from their sockets. Yaki cursed herself for not hooking her legs into the braces as the glider leveled off from the dive. Her thoughts reached upward as her eyes scanned the terrain before her. A dark blue river meandered through the waving grass. If *Fox Fire beat* back the dragons, a riverbank would be easy to find her along. Yet death could reach out of the waters come nightfall.

Someday, I will fall, and then where will you be, my child? Mother's voice whispered through her mind.

Yaki pushed it away; the Silver Fox would not die. Mother worshiped Coyote because no one else was brave enough to do so. The Silver Fox had escaped from a Lyndoner cruiser with the mustache of its captain as a trophy. Legends don't die.

However, Yaki had to confront the fact that children of legends were not always so lucky. Gently, she pulled the handle of her glider and banked toward a strand of trees far from the riverbank. She'd spend the night sheltered there and then hike south to find a buffalo herd. Where there was a herd, she'd find the nomads that roamed the plains. A gem or two would buy her a horse and a guide to get her to Lyndon.

That would work. The panic-induced thunder in her heart eased until she dared to roll the glider far enough to look up at *Fox Fire.* The huge dragon closed on the ship, less than half a league behind it. Worse, smoke streamed up from the propeller shafts. Each blade turned lazily, as if purposely allowing the dragon to catch up. At top speed, the propellers should be indistinct. "Fly faster, dammit!" she shouted as her stomach clenched. She could have helped. Murray was too busy to sing to Julia. If he hadn't kicked her off so soon… Yaki bit down on the thought and banked the other way to avoid spiraling. *Stop crying,* she told herself. *Crying never helps when you're wearing goggles.*

She scanned her surroundings and realized she was not

alone in the sky. *Always know your surroundings,* Mother chided from her mind. A dragon, slighter than the one Yaki had deflected, drifted in her direction, its wings glinting in the sunlight.

Hoping that she was just in its way, Yaki changed course, praying for it to rejoin its brother and leave her alone.

She set her sights on a new patch of trees larger than all the others, big enough to be called a proper forest. The dragons could burn it out of spite for sure, but dragon fire could burn anything out of spite. If the stories were true, their granddaddy chasing *Fox Fire* could ignite rock.

That's not helpful, she told her brain as she dived toward the grove, gaining speed at the cost of altitude. The glider's design, with the rigid frame extending beyond her head, meant the only way she could look back was to look down over her body. She could not see the dragon, but both their shadows swam over the plains' grass. The shadow's wings stayed as straight as her gliders as it narrowed the distance. Air screamed in Yaki's ears as she traded more altitude for speed. How far could the dragon's fire reach? How did the shadows translate to real distance? Questions and scary answers competed with the sensation of her blood pulsing through the space behind her eyeballs.

As the tree line zoomed closer and closer, her grimace turned into a grin. She would make it.

Heat flared around her. Time slowed and Yaki let loose a scream, but she continued flying. Had the dragon missed?

No, there was heat at her back. Dancing flames along the wings met her glance to the side. She had to land now.

Snap. The tension of her left hand disappeared as the cable went slack. The world lurched and the bright blue of the sky yawned below her as the glider's left wing dropped. Instinctively, she yanked on the remaining cable, clutching it to her heart, the flaps on the wings now in the opposite direction, Yaki's world became that of a violent spin, a nauseating alteration of blue and yellow punctuated by the distant curses streaming from her own mouth. A metallic *twang* vibrated through the wings as the second cable gave way. Already upside down, the glider lurched skyward. Yaki inhaled as she rocketed up toward the blue. For a brief moment, she hung free as the glider stalled, and she looked down. Green lay beyond her booted feet. A titter of elation cut through the fear. Had she made it?

A moment later, the nose of the string-less kite she had strapped herself to pitched over and dived toward the green canopy.

"Gods in the seven hells!" the Flower swore.

Chapter Ten

❦

The Ancients carpeted huge swaths of the land in gray stone. Beyond the Seven Saved Lands, their handiwork is everywhere. So too are the monsters. Remnants of that terrible age.

> — SEEK FIRE, CHIEF OF THE TURTLE
> CLAN OF THE LOW RIVERS TRIBE,
> LOREKEEPER

"Yakiiii!" Ishe screamed as she watched the smoking glider crash into the edge of the grove. The dragon lazily circled around his firework. Dull metal scales seemed to twinkle with smug triumph in the sunlight. She snarled at it and everyone else in the world. *Get Madria's children off first so they're sitting ducks in the sky! Brilliant, Mother!* Ishe swore as she angled her glider toward the crash site, her mind already furiously puzzling over how to deal with the dragon.

Hawk hadn't even allowed her to grab her hand cannon.

The only weapons she had were the hatchets on her back and the shells in her bandolier, both of which required letting go of the cables, which would pop her into a dangerous dive. *If only Mother has stocked Valhallan combat gliders instead.* Ishe had to leave the regrets behind as she pushed the glider well beyond its safe speed. The flimsy paper wings fluttered as they cut through the air. Once she had shed half her altitude, she leveled off and sailed toward the dragon as it wheeled around to face her. Ishe glanced down at her bandolier. A fire and a thunder shell were the last ones in easy reach; the strap that secured her to the glider hid the rest. How far had Yaki's glider been from the dragon when the flames kissed it? *Farther than I could toss a shell,* Ishe thought with rising bitterness.

The dragon was rising to meet her, charging straight for her with a leering grin on its long, stupid face. A sneer crept onto Ishe's lips as they fluttered with the force of the wind. Pulling her hands together, she took both cables in her left grip, holding the glider steady as her arm shook with the tension. With her free hand, she pulled the thunder shell and began to shake it like a bottle of celebratory fizzy cider, agitating the crystals inside. "Anybody who charges the Rhino gets the horn," she growled at the dragon, squinting as she focused intensely on the creature's maw.

As they flew closer toward each other, the shell grew increasingly warm in Ishe's hand. Details of the dragon began to resolve. Its dull gray hide wasn't uniform at all but a dappling of dark and white patches. Overall, it was much thinner than the one she'd nearly dislodged from the deck of *Fox Fire.* Its narrow head possessed a muzzle that only an alligator could love. Ishe could just make out red specks within its eye sockets as its jaw opened.

Ishe whipped the shell out in front of her. It met the gout of flame and exploded with the crack of bottled thunder. The shockwave smashed her into the glider's frame and she heard paper tear. Ishe opened her eyes in time to watch a third of her left wing fall away. Growling a curse, she seized the cables with both hands and fought to stabilize the glider as it settled into a lazy downward spiral. "Dead sails and deadwood!" Ishe filled the air around her with curses as she searched the sky for the dragon.

There it was, flying away from the grove, still shaking its head from the blast. Most importantly, Ishe still had the altitude advantage. Widening her spiral to curve around to it, Ishe angled her nose upward, gaining a few more precious feet of height as she put the sun to her back. The dragon's long neck swung side to side as it searched for her. "Gotcha now," Ishe whispered as she opened her hands. The handles nipped at her fingertips as they sprang back to the glider's frame. The contraption jerked into a steep dive as Ishe's hands flew to the Fire shell, drawing and twisting the propellant bottom off. It flared in her hand, the heat searing her skin through the leather gloves. But Ishe held it for a moment, sighting on the dragon's back before tossing it. Her aim was not impressive, but with explosions, one does not have to be dead on. The shell burst into a searing yellow light, enveloping the draft horse–sized reptile. The dragon's momentum carried it through the inferno. The majority of its tough hide, while smoking from the heat, looked none worse for wear. However, the fingers of its wings were entirely bare of their thin membranes.

Ishe laughed as the dragon tried two desperate beats of his skeletal wings before gravity took him. Rescuing her glider from the dive, she did not see the dragon hit the ground but grinned as the almost-quiet *thud* reached her ears.

The mirth faded quickly as she searched for the site of her sister's crash. The trees had seemingly swallowed the glider and girl. A fluttering in her chest grew as she circled the stand of trees, looking for the white of the paper wings. After the first pass, she glanced up in the direction of *Fox Fire,* and what she saw nearly stopped her heart entirely.

Fox Fire, her home, hung from the claws of the great black dragon, like a rabbit in the clutches of a hawk. His massive wings held both him and the ship stationary in the sky. A stream of white-winged gliders bled from the hold, seeds scattering to the wind. The dragon's long neck arched down toward the deck of the ship. The dark scales of his face shone with reflected green light, and Ishe knew from the glow that her mother still stood on the deck. The source of that light would be the Wind Slicer, like the *Fox Fire* itself, she'd never let that leave her side. Great teeth flashed as the dragon's expression changed to anger. His maw swung wide and a blue beam of energy burst from his throat. It pierced *Fox Fire,* searing through the bottom of the hull.

A keening sound tore itself from Ishe's throat. The engine room had been lanced through. Not with fire, either. The dragon let go of the ship, winging away from it. *Fox Fire* did not fall but instead shot upward like a balloon freed from its tether. Energy arced around the hull as the air filled with the high-pitched screaming whine of an overloaded ship's power crystal. Small explosions rocked the ship as sections of lift-wood spontaneously combusted, the current cooking the delicate wood. Then, as the whine reached a pitch that threatened to make Ishe's head burst like an overripe melon, an explosion tore the ship apart. For a moment, a second sun of brilliant blue drowned out all other light.

"Mama…" Ishe blinked away tears beneath her goggles. She'd been arcing the glider back and forth, shedding altitude to keep *Fox Fire* in view, and now the tops of those trees would be in touching range within moments. Her eyes scanned the treetops to no avail. "YAKI!" she called out to the forest. There was no reply.

Pulling the glider away from the trees, she prepared to land. A prayer formed on her lips as she swung her legs free of the harness: "Dear Coyote, please don't let my sister die."

Chapter Eleven

After our people huddled in the dawn of a new day, a new age, the Death Panther walked among us. Leaving gifts among our tears.

> — SEEK FIRE, CHIEF OF THE TURTLE
> CLAN OF THE LOW RIVERS TRIBE,
> LOREKEEPER, ON THE NATURE OF
> THE DEATH PANTHER

"YAKIIII!"

At the sound of her name, Yaki's eyes fluttered open. Pain filtered in along with the sunlight. She hissed at the sharp agony that lanced through her abdomen. Her mouth tasted of blood and pine. Spitting, she found a tooth chip among the splinters in her mouth. The pain in her mouth was dulled by the fact that other things hurt worse. Far worse than a beating from her mother or a tutor. Beyond the time she'd broken her leg. Still, Mother's words rose in her mind: *If it hurts, then you're not dead. If you're in good hands, relax. If you're not, then do you damnedest to get into them.*

"Yes, Mother," Yaki whimpered as she forced herself to see what was in front of her. Bark resolved. Rough, bloody bark. She had been practically making out with it. She tried to push away and found that she couldn't. Her body would not budge. A pressure and pain jerked in her chest when she did so. "No," she mouthed, and looked down. Her entire front was dark red. A branch, an inch thick, pierced her chest. A hissed breath and she could feel it in its entirety, a shaft of wood driven through her rib cage and out her back. With each breath, she felt her lungs press up against its smooth surface.

Oh, Mother and all the spirits. She gritted her teeth as a whimper escaped, and tried not to think about dying. *I'm run through. I should have never woken up,* she thought. Of course, she had heard of all sorts of gruesome injuries that sailors had survived though hope and healing crystals. This would be well beyond her little first aid crystal. "Survive," she told herself. "Survive first." That had been the point of all the lessons, whether they were dueling, dancing, or poisons. The family had to survive. She looked down again. The spike of wood had punctured her chest right below her heart.

The tree's other branches had helpfully entangled her limbs. Shifting made white-hot sparks rip through her vision. Yaki didn't have breath to scream, so she settled on a high-pitched *eeeeeeee* sound that she hissed through her teeth.,

Panting and sweating now in the chill breeze, she got her feet on the branches below her. Fresh blood had joined the old on her chest, and the metallic scent clawed at her nostrils. Yaki let her forehead rest on the bark as she studied the branch that pierced her. It was a dead-looking thing that the tree had clearly forgotten, stripped of bark and an inch thick. Easy to cut. Her hand reached down to her waist, where her rapier hung. The knife in her kit was scattered somewhere below. It would be better.

"My kingdom for a saw," she gasped as she wrapped numb fingers around the sword hilt and attempted to pull it. White stars filled with black exploded in her vision as the branch twisted inside her. The pain slapped away all the strength in her limbs and her hands fell limp at her sides. "Ahh, f-f-fuck." The guttural curse slipped from her lips as agony blotted out everything else. "Help. Somebody help me," she begged in a voice too quiet for anyone to hear. When no one answered, Yaki ground her teeth together, lips spitting every curse she knew against the pain.

She had one more voice to cry out with. The same she used to commune with the crystals. Gripping the branches near her, Yaki pushed her forehead against the rough bark.

"Please let me go," Yaki whispered to the tree that held her. "Back home, I cared for the shrine of Grandmother Willow. She talked to me sometimes, told me how the sun had changed its flavor. I could build you a shrine. I could leave you offerings every time I passed." Yaki wrapped her hand around the base of the branch that held her, and willed it to break. Begged it to set her free. "Please, I'm willing to bargain. My mother needs me. My family will be paupers without me." Yaki wheezed, talking if only to think of something other than the pain and the blood.

"YAKI!"

Hope surged through her heart as Ishe's voice boomed through the forest, so much so that Yaki felt it beating against the branch in her chest.

"Ishe," Yaki tried to answer, but her lungs only yielded an urgent whisper.

"Yaki, where are you?!" Ishe's voice came again.

"Here! I'm here!" Yaki's voice barely managed a whisper,

and kicked at the tree to vent her frustration. The jostle made pain erupt anew.

"Yaki!" Ishe's voice now sounded farther away.

"I hate you!" Yaki hissed at the tree before extending herself in every direction. "Please, anyone that can hear me. Please free me now! Let me reach my sister and my mother. I'll leave offerings of our spoils. I'll give service if I survive. I'll brand your name and image on my body, which is clean and pure. Just give me the strength to reach my sister!" Hot tears seemed to burn her cheeks as she made her oath.

Stillness settled over the forest as if the trees were suddenly afraid to breathe. Yaki felt hot breath on the back of her neck. A voice crept into her ears: "I hear you as you wither, Flower."

"Who?" Yaki's word came out as a breathy cloud of white mist.

The shadows stirred and moon-pale eyes opened above her. The blackness shifted and a cat the size of a lion encircled the tree trunk, lounging on branches so thin, they would scarcely bear the weight of a sparrow. Her body seemed composed of night itself, stars twinkling in her plush coat. "Only I could hear such a tiny plea."

Ishe felt what little warmth she had fleeing her body. There were not many panthers in Sparrow's stories, but this was neither Cougar nor Bobcat. No, the Low Rivers' spirit of the end itself had deigned to hear her, the Death Panther. She revealed herself once and once only. The pain in Yaki's chest faded as she drew closer.

"Please. I meant what I said," Yaki pleaded as a dark paw reached out toward her. She leaned her head back to avoid its touch.

"I am no Oni, child. I cannot be bargained with nor bought. However, I am sated with the blood of your family for now. Today, I bring you a gift." The paw turned upward like a hand, and a vibrant green seed lay on the pad. "This will give you the strength to reach your sister. She will determine the length of your life."

Yaki took the seed; it radiated warmth through her fingertips and made her entire hand pulse with a beat stronger than the one in her chest. In the stories, it always paid to give respect to spirits, so Yaki chose her next words with care. "You honor me with this, although I do not know your proper name or mark. I ask to know your mark so I might honor you as long as I walk between the earth and sky."

The cat blinked slowly, and a low purr rolled forth from her shadowy body. "Then I will give you my mark to wear." Yaki felt something very hot brush her shoulder blade, searing into her skin and bone. Despite the scent of cooked pork, no pain came.

"Thank you," Yaki whispered, and swallowed the seed. The warmth fell down through the dark of her body and exploded with a flame that rekindled her waning heart. The thunderous rhythm sent blood coursing through her like an untamed river. The gray of the world snapped back to vibrant color.

Grabbing hold of the branch, she snapped it at its base with a turn of her wrist. An echoing *crack* cascaded around the forest. The cat had vanished from sight, but Yaki could still feel her in the quiet of the forest.

"Yaki!" Ishe's voice sounded closer this time.

There was no time to waste. Yaki picked her way down the tree and stumbled toward her sister's voice.

Chapter Twelve

The healers of the ancients trained for decades. Now there are only the priests who declare that if the crystals cannot fix you, then you are not worth saving.

— HON NISHAMURA, CHIEF
HISTORIAN OF THE STEWARD, FROM
HIS PRIVATE JOURNALS

"YAKI!" ISHE SHOUTED. HER THROAT FELT RAW AND abused by screaming, so she yelled again, "Yaki!" to teach her throat a lesson about being weak at a time like this. If Mother was dead, Yaki couldn't be. The Flower wouldn't leave the Rhino alone. Not at a time like this. Ishe wiped her eyes, still seeing that blue fireball in the sky. Surely the Lyndoners had seen that! Airships would be on their way to gather the scattered crew any moment now. She just had to find Yaki. With the Flower's looks and the Rhino's everything else, they'd own the city within weeks. So what if the crew thought they were stupid children? They'd show them all.

"Yaki!" Ishe bellowed, turning in place. The trees around her looked the same as all the others. She hadn't seen a single trace of Yaki's glider. Not that she'd been seeing anything clearly since the blast. The afterimage of *Fox Fire*'s destruction still floated in her vision. The tears hadn't helped either; at least those had finally run out.

Slow down and think, Ishe, she told herself. *What would Mother do, other than face a dragon with nothing but a crystal-boosted letter opener? Think about the spaces where Yaki could have crashed relative to her own landing.*

"Ishe." The voice came on the wind, so faint that Ishe mistook it for a thought and dismissed it. She was imagining the forest from above. How she should have been searching the forest instead of wandering aimlessly, calling her name. Yaki had to be unconscious and unable to answer her.

"Ishe!" A little louder now. She screwed her eyes shut, pondering the problem. She had no idea where she was within the circular forest, but if she walked to the edge, she could look at nearby landmarks. The river lay south and an even larger forest lay north.

"Ishe!" *Yaki's voice!*

Finally opening her eyes, Ishe saw a figure staggering toward her, bracing itself against the tree trunks. Ishe's feet were carrying her toward her sister before her exhausted mind had even begun to catch up. Branches whipped at her face as she charged. Ishe mentally took back every mean thing she had said about her sister and spread her arms wide in the final stretch, fully intending to squeeze Yaki within an inch of her life.

"Stop!" Yaki held out a hand and Ishe stumbled to a halt, her speed forcing her to grab hold of a sapling to stop in time. Only then did she see beyond the slim shape of her sister: the blood-soaked clothes, the swollen and broken nose, and, as Yaki leaned toward her, she saw the half a foot of wood protruding from her sister's back. A mortal wound if she had ever seen one. "Ishe, help me," Yaki's voice squeezed out before her knees buckled.

"Don't you dare." Ishe flung herself forward to catch the falling girl by her shoulders and hauled her to her feet. Yaki's head lolled. Her pupils were narrowed to pinholes. "What happened to you?" Ishe said as she desperately looked for a safe place to lay her sister down. Her eyes hooked on the jagged shaft of wood protruding from her sister's chest.

Carefully, Ishe laid Yaki down on the ground on her side, trying not to jostle the stick. Then she took her sister's hand and felt for a pulse. Slow, but there.

"I'm not dead yet. I promise," Yaki managed with the weakest of smiles.

Ishe swallowed down Mother's fate. That story would kill her sister as surely as a knife. Fumbling with her pack, Ishe took out the small first aid crystal and closed Yaki's fingers around it. It began to glow softly in the shadowed light of the forest. Sundown was coming. The crystal wouldn't last long, but it would dull the pain a little and contain the bleeding. "I'm going to take it out."

Yaki closed her eyes and grimaced.

"We're at least a day's walk from Lyndon. I'll have to tie you to my back. If we're lucky, we'll meet a plains tribe on the way. Good or bad luck, I don't know. Can't have that stuck in you while moving." Ishe babbled as she took what little she had for bandages and divided them into two equal piles. Standing, she peered at the branch protruding from Yaki's back. It was as straight as you could hope for with a bloodthirsty tree, with only a slight kink in the wood. However, the tip was a jagged thing. It would have to come out the same way it went in.

Cutting open Yaki's shirt revealed a wound that made Ishe suck in air through her teeth. The stick punched to the right of her sternum. "Good thing you're not droopy like Mom, or this stick would have hit the bull's-eye," Ishe said as she wrapped her fingers around the shaft.

The world went dark for a half second and then the setting sun came back. Ishe froze like a hare being watched. The dragon. Retrieving the body of the one she'd burnt the wings off of? Dragons weren't supposed to care about their young. She pushed the thought away. Yaki first.

"What are you waiting for? Get it over with. I refuse to die with this thing in me," Yaki whispered with an encouraging amount of strength.

Taking a deep breath and blowing out her cheeks with the exhale, Ishe placed one hand, fingers spread wide on the swollen flesh, and took a firmer grip on the branch. "Breathe out," she instructed, willing her hammering heart to still along with her trembling hands. The wood resisted at first but soon yielded, slipping from the wound as if oiled. Dark blood swelled out of the holes at either side, and Ishe pressed her two pads of gauze to them, praying they'd be enough.

"Thank, you Ishe," Yaki whispered. "I can sleep now."

"No, you don't. Sleep is the last thing you need now. You're going to sit up and hold this front bandage while I tape the back one down." She pressed harder on the wounds.

An animal whimper escaped Yaki. "Ishe," she whined.

"Don't you know you can't argue with the Rhino? Sit up, Flower," Ishe growled.

Yaki obeyed, pushing herself up and panting with pain. She was breathing easier, at least. Her hand fumbled until she took control of the front bandage. One hand free, Ishe pulled open the back of her sister's shirt. On the left shoulder blade stood the raised impression of a large cat's paw as if the pads had been burned in a long time before.

"You're going to have to be real careful with those dresses once we get to Lyndon." Ishe kept her tone conversational. Most of Sparrow's stories of cats featured them as single-minded brutes, but if one had saved her sister, she'd happily revise that impression. "Big ol' mark right on your shoulder," Ishe said before peeling a strip of tape from the roll with her teeth.

Yaki gave a coughing chuckle. "You're going to be the pretty one after this, Ishe. Between a flattened nose and a mark, nobody will want a mutt from the Golden Hills. Mother will give you the dowry and I'll play maidservant. Maybe I'll take *Fox Fire* once you have a babe in your belly." There was a slight edge to Yaki's voice, her tone wavering.

"*Fox Fire*'s really damaged. She's limping into port as we speak." Yaki finished taping the bandage to the pale skin. Dark red blood threatened to intrude on the edges already.

"She left us behind?" Yaki's breath hitched.

"Only temporarily. She's a captain first. We're crew." Ishe pushed the blue fireball back into the depths of her mind. "We'll meet her in Lyndon." Ishe hurried to Yaki's front and knelt.

The world went dark and cold, another half-second eclipse.

"What was that?" Yaki asked.

"Dragon. It's circling." Ishe pulled Yaki's cold hands away and taped the bandage to her chest. "Now keep holding that. I'll get the back." Ishe stole a look at her sister's face. The deathly pale skin held slightly unfocused eyes, but that was an improvement. Some tribes held Cougar as a healer. Could she have left the mark? Animal medicine was a fickle thing to rely on, for city dwellers.

Ishe filled time, telling Yaki the story of how she'd downed the dragon on her tail as she hugged Yaki close. Taking off her flight jacket, she slipped it around Yaki's body and buttoned her in. The last embers of the sun died away and the forest around them became a nest of shadows and pale silver light. Try as she might, the cold seeped into her arms and legs, and her teeth began to chatter. Once her jaws started, the rest of her body joined in. Yaki, in her arms, was either growing colder or simply leeching more heat than Ishe's body had to give.

There was nothing for it. The cold would kill them before either the dragons or the wildlings in the river had a chance. Gathering wood proved to be a much longer affair than she'd hoped, but there were plenty of dry sticks to kindle the fire.

Once lit, the fire was a hungry little thing. Ishe stayed up, half-expecting the dragon to crash down on her, but no gigantic talons reached down from the forest canopy.

At one point, she blinked and daylight filtered through the trees within the space of a perceived second. The fire crackled merrily away beside a slumbering Yaki. An icicle of panic receded from Ishe's heart when her chest rose.

Ishe pulled one of the pemmican biscuits from her tin of supplies, broke off a piece, and sucked on it. Wincing at the taste, she pushed herself up, intending to wake Yaki. Her color had gone from corpse-pale to a fevered flush through the night. Ishe reached out to touch her forehead and snatched her fingers back from the burning skin. The bleeding had stopped, but the chest was a mass of angry, swollen tissue.

Only after Ishe slapped her cheeks did Yaki's eyes creak open. "Ishe? Where's Mother?"

Ishe held out her canteen. "You need to drink some water."

A swallow of water produced a coughing fit that subsided into a near-silent howl of pain. "Hurts," Yaki gasped.

Ishe found the healing crystal in the dirt nearby, its surface clouded and cracked, completely spent. There would be nothing for it. Ishe had hoped that whatever freed Yaki might ward off the infection, too, but no such luck.

"Yaki." Ishe splashed a bit of water on Yaki's face until her brown eyes focused. "You have to invoke your new friend again. Ask him or her to clean away the infection."

"Didn't ask for that. Just didn't want to die in that tree." The eyes closed. "She said…said it's up to you now."

"Bloody iron and deadwood, Yaki! Don't you fucking die on me," Ishe growled.

Yaki's eyes remained half-open and her grip slack, but she gave a small smirk. "Trying…" At least she continued to breathe. With a grunt, Ishe hauled Yaki's delicate form up over her shoulders and began to slog north. Ishe was stouter, taller, and stronger than her hour-older sister, but still exhausted. All she could do was continue putting one foot in front of the other.

Chapter Thirteen

✧❖✧

Dragons are simple. The bigger they are, the harder they are to kill. I can only imagine that fighting the Grand Wyrm would have been like fighting an erupting volcano.

> — SHINTO YASAMOTO, AUTHOR OF
> DRAGON HUNTING WITHOUT DYING

THE EDGE OF THE FOREST SNEAKED UP ON ISHE, HER total concentration consumed in moving and focused on her feet. So, when she stepped out into the direct midmorning sunlight, it nearly blinded her. She stood there blinking stupidly for a moment before stepping back into the shade of the tree line. Yaki moaned with delirium as she was set against a tree. Still breathing, at least. Ishe pulled at the back of her shirt, plastered to her from the combined sweat of both siblings. She forced water down Yaki's throat before allowing herself a swig.

A circle of crystal-blue sky yawned overhead, as if the

Daylight himself had punched a hole through the thick cloud cover. Beneath the cloud, a haze of precipitation obscured the lands beyond it. The bulbous hull of a small merchant ship hung like a brown moon near the outer edge of the nice day. Smaller skiffs were winging away from a hanger on the side. A salvage ship? Hope propelled Ishe forward a step until she caught sight of another shape lazily circling up to it on a thermal. At this distance, one could easily mistake it for a vulture or condor, but the shape of those wings belonged to no bird. Ishe watched as the dragon climbed above the ship before gracefully gliding to its deck.

Dragons and humans worked together to hunt *Fox Fire*? Why? What had Mother done? Who were these people who were stupid enough to serve a dragon? That would end precisely how the Great Wyrm's Empire had ended: in fire. Shaking her head in disbelief, Ishe scanned the sky for any more enemies, and saw none. The only thing that would have survived the explosion of *Fox Fire* would be the crew itself.

Ishe's hand fingered her empty hand-cannon holster. She had a hatchet, a knife, and three more shells, but that was it for weapons. Nothing for it. The ship would attract attention from local tribes, and the larger forest would be teeming with scouts before too long. They'd speak trade if nothing else. The forest stood maybe two miles off, through the rolling grass. If she didn't step on a rattler or worse, they'd be home free. Hoisting Yaki back onto her shoulders, Ishe set her sights on the distant green and started off.

The grass crunched underfoot in a steady rhythm, the stalks around her whispering in the morning breeze. "Hang on, Yaki. Just hang on" were the only words that broke the song of the grasshoppers that flitted away from her trudging boots. At the halfway point, a spot between her shoulder blades began to itch with the ferocity of a bedbug bite. At intervals, her pace quickened and slowed, as wariness battled a growing dread that she had been spotted.

A bass *swoosh* signaled the end. A great shadow passed overhead and a column of flame swept across her path, igniting the field before her.

Ishe did not stop. That was exactly what the dragon wanted her to do. A little voice screamed inside her head to think about it as the temperature rose around them. She paused only long enough to pull the last ice shell she possessed from her belt. With a flick of the wrist, she tossed it forward into a patch of burning brush. The shell exploded in an icy blast, snuffing out the flames before her. Ishe continued on as the dragon dived low toward her right, scorching another line in the field even as the crystalline blades of frozen grass shattered beneath her feet.

Biting her lip, Ishe waited for the blast of flame to hit her directly as she watched the shadow circle around the field like a creature beneath the surface of the ground. Instead, the huge creature glided into her field of vision. The earth trembled beneath Ishe's feet the moment it touched down, as if shivering in revulsion. The great wings folded away and the creature stood, towering over the forest she had sought to hide in. A spitting image of Yaz'noth, the Horned Serpent, watched her with golden eyes; his scales, said to be composed of heavy black iron, shone in the sun. Rusty red patches dappled the back of his neck. He sat as a dog might, if a dog were more than eight stories tall. His long, sinuous tail stretched out across Ishe's path, the very tip lazily curling and uncurling. Waiting for her.

Pausing to adjusting her grip, Ishe heard her sister moan. "I wish you'd wake up, Yaki," Ishe told her. "Might need some of those honeyed words from school." Then, feeling like a mouse facing a cat, she walked on as if the dragon would move.

The dragon did not growl or threaten. He did not do anything but watch as Ishe approached him. With each step she took, he loomed larger. His tail alone would be a two-story clamber, but the dragon's hide was not some sort of shadow. They were composed of large overlapping diamond-shaped plates, and Ishe reckoned they were thick enough to provide hand- and footholds. As she closed, he shifted, lying down and arching his long neck toward her. There was no mistaking the shape of the head. The slender antlers branched out from the brow, shining blades of steel that protruded along a jaw that could snap up half a classroom's worth of children in one great gulp. Or so they said at the finishing school when they dined beneath the dead eyes of this same face in the Steward's hall. The head cocked slightly, studying her with eyes that outweighed her and then some. The stink of his sulfurous breath flooded Ishe's nostrils and made her cough.

Still, there were differences from the head that hung in the hall beyond this one's being attached to the rest of a dragon. No scars disrupted the smooth scales of the face. The horns were not quite as thick, and the corners of this one's muzzle were upturned, giving it the appearance of a sly smile. It was a disturbingly human expression on such a beast.

Ishe did not know what to do, so she continued. Only once she closed to several arms' lengths did the dragon speak. "Touch me without permission and I will kill you both." The voice, deep and full of gravel, contained no hint of anger, the quiet authority of one used to being obeyed. Ishe turned sharply, making to walk around the tail's length. The tail, however, curled, whispering through the grass, so if she followed its length, she'd walk directly into the dragon's maw.

Seeing no avenue of escape, Ishe turned and faced the eyes that burned with a curiosity dragons were not supposed to possess. "Let us go..." Ishe swallowed. "...please." In her mind, she saw the fatal strike that had destroyed *Fox Fire* replayed. He'd given Madria time to watch her death come. A long moment of helplessness stretched. Ishe steeled herself as she slipped a Fire shell from her belt. If she had to go, she and Yaki would go on their own terms.

The dragon's eyes narrowed fractionally but did not seem terribly distraught. "I'm afraid your freedom and anyone else's aboard *Fox Fire* will require far more than a please or thank you."

"You've already taken both *Fox Fire* and our mother." Ishe swallowed down the bile in her throat as her fist tightened on the shell.

The smile broadened, displaying a glint of steel teeth behind the thin lips. "You are the daughters of the Silver Fox, then. I thought so. There is a resemblance in your scent. You're the one they call Little Rhino, and, on your back, the dying one must be the Flower."

"We are," Ishe admitted, internally cursing herself for giving up information. She could hear the teachers from conversation class screaming in the back of her mind. "I don't know what Mother did to upset you, but surely the score is settled now that you've ruined us."

A rueful chuckle rolled from the dragon's maw. "Oh, no, poor thing. You're very wrong. When dealing with such short-lived creatures as humans, I take a multigenerational approach. Punishment falls to those who betray me. Repayment is the task of the sons and daughters. The system needs to work that way. Otherwise, humans tend to be short-sighted."

"Pity on you, then. We're the last of our line and I won't let you take us." Ishe held the shell up in front of her as if it were a holy symbol warding off the mad dead. She'd have to drop Yaki to arm it, but the dragon lacked any means to snatch it from her hands.

"Yes, I see that, clever little monkey. A great flaw in my plan has been spotted. Whatever shall I do?" That awful chuckle rolled out of his muzzle. Ishe stood still, frozen in indecision. Fortunately, the dragon continued. "Now, I suppose in the context of all, that I have to make atoning for your mother's insult preferable to death. Don't I, hmm?" His gaze shifted a fraction from Ishe's face to Yaki's limp form. The dragon inhaled through his nostrils, the grass bowing in his direction. "I assume there is some fondness for your sister? After all, I believe your plan was to carry her all the way to Lyndon."

"You can't have her," Ishe snapped, turning so her body sheltered the smaller girl.

"No one will in a few hours. Not with that fever and infection. Less time if you explode that shell. I can prevent that. I might be able to cure her entirely. Your sister's health for the return of what your mother stole from me. Then you and your sister, along with the entire crew of *Fox Fire*, will be free to make your own way. I'll even say that I don't need further recompense for poor Brindle and Wipple, poor Brindle having finally spoken his first words just last month." A curl of smoke escaped from the dragon's nostril even as his smile grew wider.

"The quicksilver is already at the refinery in the Golden Hills," Ishe said.

"And who better to sneak in and retrieve it than a rumored bastard child of the Steward?" He grinned in full, displaying teeth longer than swords.

Ishe stepped back from the deadly shine and sputtered. Thoughts tumbled together. Oaths she had sworn since childhood to protect the Hills and their Steward, but also her mother's vicious rows with him during her days as a "favored" concubine. But one voice rose among the others.

Her mother's mantra, "Family comes first." She gathered herself.

"If Yaki survives and returns to health, then I will fetch you your quicksilver," Ishe announced.

The great tail uncurled, revealing the world beyond it, and the dragon rumbled with pleasure. "Allow me to clear some room for her." He rose up onto all fours, the earth itself groaning under the weight. The massive shoulders rolled as a visible bulge began to travel up his neck. Twisting his head to the side, his mouth opened to disgorge a torrent of metal objects, they clattered to the ground. A massive pile of blades, gizmos, and shell-thrower barrels reached nearly to the height of Ishe's jaw, which hung open.

"I'll need some specialized equipment once we return home. But…" The dragon trailed off as his eyes narrowed in concentration. A deep gurgling echoed from inside his chest, and he exhaled a torrent of white smoke. "There, that will keep her alive. Give her here." He extended his head and his jaws yawned open before her. The wide tongue looked to be made of asphalt, wide enough that both Ishe and Yaki could lie on it without touching.

Ishe's mouth worked until a sound came out. "You—You can't eat her!"

"I won't eat her. Dragons don't eat humans. We eat minerals and metals. Preferably refined iron seasoned with a dash of steel." The dragon's voice echoed from farther down his throat, as if there were a man in his stomach doing all the talking. "She's going to my forge, where I will repair her damaged body. I do this for my followers occasionally. It's quite an honor. In a few days, she will be returned whole, if not entirely happy."

"Last time I checked, nobody comes out of a stomach whole." Ishe took a step back.

The dragon closed his maw, shook his head, and tutted.

"Do they not even teach basic dragon anatomy anymore?" He chuckled, embodying a level of smugness that made Ishe's fingers curl. "My forge is not my stomach. It's a staging area and much more." He nodded at the pile of metal objects. "I made those within it. Now give her to me." Again, he opened his mouth and waited.

Ishe sucked in a breath and eyed the pile of goods. They all shone as if new, although in various stages of completion. Some of the blades, in particular, looked far too wide. Still, nothing looked digested. Ishe swallowed.

"If this is a joke, you are exceptionally cruel." Ishe pulled Yaki from her shoulder and carried her forward. The heat of the fever had grown. Steam rose from her sweat-soaked clothing. Every voice in her head yammered at Ishe to stop, but she saw no other course of action. Yaki's life was melting away. Her chest trembled with every labored breath as Ishe stepped over the massive row of teeth and planted her foot on the inside of the dragon's maw. Damp, not like a mouth but the interior of a cave. She paused, waiting for the teeth to snap closed on her body.

Yet only one part of the mouth moved: the tip of the tongue flipped upward in a very lewd come-hither gesture. "Put her in the center and step out," the dragon instructed with the tone of a bored file clerk as if Yaki was nothing more than a bland rice bun.

"Sorry, Yaki," Ishe murmured in her sister's ear as she lay her on the road-like tongue. As she stepped back out, the mouth closed behind her, and the sound of a long, deep swallow filled the air.

"Perfectly flavored!" the dragon exclaimed.

Ishe whirled, her fist swinging out in a wild hook. It only hit air as the dragon's head snapped back out of range.

"Kidding! I'm joking! She is fine." The dragon grinned.

"Well, not fine. She's almost dead, but I'll try to fix that now."

"You! You— You!" Ishe stammered, choking on sudden rage.

"Am terrible? I'm not surprised you think so. All that dragon-slaying propaganda they babble on about in your city. I am the Horned Serpent, Yaz'noth. Scourge of the Spine!" he boomed, then looked down at her and squinted in confusion. "You should be kneeling now."

Ishe fell to her knees, not so much out of fear but sheer bewilderment. She had feared dragons as massive engines of destruction. Sinister plotters of the downfall of mankind. But now she had the dawning realization that this massive creature that three hundred years before had nearly shattered her city was madder than old Lady Yakamoto at the palace.

"Good girl!" Yaz'noth's tone pitched high. "Wait there for a moment and we'll get you some nice chains that fit for the ride home."

What have I done? Ishe thought as she finally noticed the squad of men marching toward her.

Chapter Fourteen

❧

Death needs life. The Death Panther understands this.

— SEEK FIRE, CHIEF OF THE TURTLE
CLAN OF THE LOW RIVERS TRIBE,
LOREKEEPER, ON THE NATURE OF
THE DEATH PANTHER

THE FLOWER FOUND HERSELF IN A DARKNESS THAT HAD never been pierced by a ray of sun. The pain of her wounds had not followed her. Was this death? Had Ishe not been able to save her? This had to be the void beyond life. Funny; she had always imagined the other side to be cold like the corpses she helped push off the deck of *Fox Fire*. Instead, she found it warm, even soft as it cradled her body. The blackness moved around her, and she felt muscle shift beneath it. Something warm and rough scraped up her leg, which suddenly flared in pain. Flower tried to scream but the blackness held her, stifling sound in her throat as hard, sharp things pressed around her knee. Agony illuminated the blackness with dark light. No void was this; the Death Panther encircled her, her coat darker than despair and her giant muzzle clapped down over Ishe's knee.

The Panther's eyes were closed as if in concentration. The Flower felt her teeth sink deeper, beyond the flesh of the leg, each of the knife-sized fangs reaching into her heart. Memories sparked in the darkness. She heard her mother call within her mind: "Protect my Little Flower."

Then the terrible pulling sensation began. It allowed her one single scream and she made the best of it, letting loose a shrill crescendo of pure agony as she felt herself begin to tear at the seams. *Pop, pop, pop.* The sound echoed in her ears like the cracks of cannon fire, each one firing another memory into her mind. The silk of her first dress, accompanied by her mother's smile. *My little flower.* The sharp sting of her dance instructor's tongue, flavored with the bite of her long nails. *This is your left side, Flower! Now do it right!* Mama paddling her bottom for accidentally slicing her hand open with broken glass. *No scars, Flower! None! You must be pristine!* Endlessly the memories came, every time anyone had called her Flower. *My Flower, little bud, pretty little Flower.* So many at once, good memories, sad memories, they all hurt.

Panting, she opened her eyes to look into her own frightened face. Not a mirror but an apparition of herself sitting in the jaws of a massive cat, her fur black, her fangs obsidian. On second glance, the girl was different from Yaki: her eyes larger, her skin unmarred, her figure beyond thinness, stretching into delicate. Clothed in the finest dress Yaki had ever seen before. Blood pulsed from a fist-sized hole in her chest, pouring down the fabric and leaving it unstained. Her name was Flower, the girl that Yaki had been sculpted into all her life.

"You have honored me and are worthy of my gifts, daughter of the Silver Fox." The voice of the Death Panther floated through the void. "I gave you life. My second gift is death. I take the Flower instead of you."

The jaws snapped closed. The girl shattered like glass.

Chapter Fifteen

❦

It's a rare dragon who will talk to a human. After all, do you apologize to a nest of hornets before you set it on fire?

— SHINTO YASAMOTO, AUTHOR OF
DRAGON HUNTING WITHOUT DYING

THEY CALLED THEMSELVES THE DRAGONSWORN. ALL OF them could have walked into the Golden Hills without raising a fuss if not for their shaven heads. Their skin had a golden highlight compared to her own ruddy complexion, but they were slim and delicate, as if they had gone underfed their entire lives. Their leader spoke in barking commands. "Come!" "Kneel!" "Present wrists!" Ishe gave him no trouble. In the minutes after Yaki had disappeared down the dragon's gullet, exhaustion had settled onto her mind. The battle she fought was one to stay on her feet as she was herded back toward their waiting boats. Thoughts of resistance did not kindle until she was on board the small freighter. Already chained to a bed in an empty bunkroom, she saw it was a little late for dramatic escapes. She had a vague hope that the crew from *Fox Fire* would join her, but none appeared, to both her relief and concern.

Mostly, she slept. In the haze of half-remembered nightmares, she saw the burning ball of blue fire again and again and Yaki's muffled screams echoing out between Yaz'noth's grinning teeth. After wakefulness came, a slip of a girl brought her ship's biscuits and water. A stern guard watched from the door. They spoke Golden with a sort of bubbly accent but in the most formal of tones in her presence.

Inquires were met with a polite shake of the head, a refusal to answer. All except one. The crew was safe and fed. Requests to see them were ignored. Ishe could not bring herself to force the issue. She had laid Yaki on the tongue of the beast that had shattered their home centuries before. It made her heart burn and her stomach churn, although she saw no other way she could have acted to save her sister. The sensation of betrayal and loss bound her more surely than the chains around her wrists. Hawk would be captain now. A captain without a ship, but it would be her they answered. If Hawk had allowed herself to be captured at all. It had been whispered that both Hawk and Sparrow could change into their namesakes. But where would that have left poor Blinky? Sparrow wouldn't have left him behind, would he? That thought hurt. All of it hurt. Had she not charged the dragon on the deck, would things be different? She hadn't even gotten to fire the elemental lance! They had been hours away from Lyndon. They had to have seen the dragon's predation from the city. Why had they not sent help?

With too many thoughts and nothing to do with them, Ishe lay down on her wooden berth and tried not to think.

"WE HAVE ARRIVED," THE SAME MAN WHO HAD collected Ishe from the grass-covered plain announced two days later. He had appeared at the door as Ishe had been counting the number of nails above her for the hundredth time. The air had become cool enough that her breath was visible by the dim crystals that lit the room. He wore breeches and a brown woolen jacket, done up with ribs made of polished bone. Ishe recognized the utilitarian design from the illuminated history books she had copied in school, the uniform of a soldier of the Grand Wyrm's Empire. Rank was indicated by a number of golden talons on his shoulder, positioned so it could be easily seen by creatures of a much larger size. This man had two pips. He undid the chain around her wrist and presented her with a fur-lined cloak. Ishe draped it around her shoulders before the man herded her out the door and into a narrow corridor where other Dragonsworn were running to and fro. All yielded to the two-pip man. Nobody else had any pips at all.

The lungful of air that greeted Ishe on the deck bit her throat and tasted thin. If the ship had a crystal for keeping the crew alive for higher altitudes, its range did not extend to the deck. They floated among the white-capped peaks of mountains jagged like teeth; Ishe recognized the mountains of the Spine, if not their location within it.

"We are less than a day's sail from the Golden Hills," the man said, seeming to read her thoughts.

"And what is this place?" Ishe wrapped the cloak around herself, trying to guard against the air's frosty sting. The ship idled in the shadow of a snowy peak as the sun began to peek over the rise. A dock shaped much like a tongue, its edges rounded, extended from a large cave entrance. She saw the structure was perfectly shaped to fold back into the arch of the cave. Above it, a bundle of canvas flapped in the breeze; camouflage for the entrance when not in use? If they were only a half-day's sail from the Golden Hills, then they had been living under the Navy's nose for...centuries. Surely, someone would have defected or found them in that time?

"It is the Lord's design." The Dragonsworn tapped his chest twice with his fist before beckoning her to the railing. Peering over, Ishe felt her heart unclench a tiny bit as she recognized the gray, plain clothes of the crew of *Fox Fire*. Wrists chained behind their backs, they marched two by two down a ramp that extended from the middle of the ship's hull. "They will work the mines until they either swear the oath, die, or other."

Ishe's heart made a dive for her spleen. "I understood one of those options."

The man nodded. "I am named Goru. Among the Dragonsworn, I have two talons. The highest at the moment is three. I have quarters all to myself and may share them with who I wish."

Ishe neck made several pops as her head swiveled toward him. She found the barest hint of a smarmy smirk on his lips as he half-raised a hand to ward off any blow.

"Something to keep in mind after the Master is done with...whatever he does. If you do not please him, you will be either dead or forgotten. My name could save you from the mines in the case you're forgotten." His gaze lingered for a moment on her chest before turning back toward the prisoners. All it would take would be a foot sweep and a push, and the man would be hurtling toward his death on the rocks below.

"You didn't answer my questions," she pointed out.

"Not my place to answer them. Answers can change," he said with a disgusting amount of confidence.

Ishe was about to comment on that when a set of broad shoulders caught her eye. Hawk walked with an unhurried stride as if she chose to be there, her head held high as

Sparrow hunched in her shadow. Yet he held his hand out to his side, fingers splayed wide. *Stay,* those fingers said. Ishe saw no sign of the eight eyes the message was usually intended for. *Had the spider stowed away on the ship?* Her eyes swept the gangplank for some sign but caught no movement. Had Mother been the only one who went up with the ship?

She watched the pair disappear into the darkness of the mountain. She had not seen Murray, the engineer, nor his scrawny sidekicks, Jack and Jill, but she did spot Koshue, the expert gunner, among the crew.

"It's your turn. We will get you presentable for the Master. Maybe food other than ship's biscuit." Goru indicated the ladder with a jerk of his chin.

Chapter Sixteen

The ancients had this absurd idea that pain stopped after death. Perhaps it is their lack of care for their ancestors that spurred on their end.

— HON NISHAMURA, CHIEF
HISTORIAN OF THE STEWARD'S
ARCHIVES

PAIN. PAIN INTERSPERSED WITH MOMENTS OF SHEER agony. That's where Yaki existed. Something long and hard impaled her throat and forced her to breathe. Her lungs ached each time it forced hot air into her. She had awoken as something unseen slit her open lengthwise. Smoke from her own burning flesh crawled up into the still air of her nostrils. Then countless things slid into her chest, long, wriggly things. In this horrible way, she discovered the shape of everything inside of her. The things wrapped around every organ and vessel her chest contained. Her heart and lungs strained against their bonds. A new spear of agony lanced through her as the things brushed the wall of her heart. She writhed as they worried at it, like tongues poking at the shattered stump of a tooth.

A wet rip vibrated through her as something pulled free. The things recoiled as wetness bloomed within her chest. A merciful blackness reached up to claim her.

Light. A hellish red glow burned against Yaki's eyelids as she fluttered back into consciousness. Everything she had left remained. The tube down her throat and the horrible invasion of things reached inside her, squeezing. She did not hear a heartbeat. Instead, she felt the blood push through her veins with the squeezing of the thing inside her chest. Dimly, she wondered what this thing could be that first forced her to breathe and now propelled her very blood through her body. What had she done to deserve this torture? Her mind reached out for the Death Panther, pleading for her to save Yaki from this. Her mental touch brushed the cat's fur, but the Death Panther did not answer the plea.

Cracking open her eyes, Yaki found her head immobilized. The origin of the light stayed out of her gaze, but it illuminated the space around her. Long, flat strips of a substance that glinted like wet stone hung down in front her. One of the things had coiled into a tube that reached down her throat. At the base of it, maybe a foot away from her eyes, a half dozen of the strips formed two sacks that inflated and deflated with the rhythm of her breathing. Beyond that, she could see several more coils of the things. These were a variety of sizes and reached into her chest, flexing and releasing with the movement of the blood in her veins.

Beyond those, nearer to the light, more of the strange tentacles writhed, making the shadows dance. Every once in a while, a lump of something bright with heat would be carried up into her vision. The tentacles alternated between striking like pistons and squeezing the substance, which Yaki dimly recognized as metal. Between bright flashes in the glow, disks of metal gave way to gears. Eventually, the glow faded, but Yaki could still hear the steady rustle as the blind things continued to work.

She glided through the haze of half-sleep, twitching awake when something shifted inside of her. How much longer? How long at it been? Time and pain stretched against each other like the taffy sold in the northern cities where sugarcane grew.

The light came again. This time, a mass of tentacles pushed up from the floor where she had been entombed and formed a shelf of molten metal. Angled so she could watch, the thinnest manipulators dipped into the pool and drew out long strands of metal, which others would take and pull longer into a fine wire. After five spools, complete with needles, had been made, the far wall of the chamber came alive with a rippling movement. The center of it opened as a large oval shape joined her in the chamber. The tentacles fell on it like a mass of ravenous snakes. A crack sounded, a sharp keen of pain, and then silence. An object was lifted up, just a little bigger than Yaki's fist. It gleamed of silver and gold in the red light. Tubes stretched out from it, constructed from the same coiled tentacles that surrounded her and were inside her.

The object was brought over to the shelf, in reach of the finest tentacles that had made the wire. Crystals, a dozen of tiny red shards, were attached to the surface of the thing, welded into place by melted metal. The last piece to be attached wasn't a crystal. It was a misshapen lump the size of a mouse. It squirmed as the tentacles sewed it to the back of the thing.

Once that last stitch was tied, the thing began to tick.

Then twitch. Its sides pulsed before settling into a steady rhythm. *Ka-chink. Ka-chink. Ka-chink.*

No, Yaki thought as she slowly realized the identity of the thing before her. Muscles twitched futilely and her diaphragm spasmed as she fought to squeeze lungs that she no longer controlled and scream. Her eyes widened slightly, the only outward expression of the agony she achieved as the tentacles wrenched her chest open to lower the metal heart into her.

Chapter Seventeen

There is nothing so irresistible to a dragon than a bar of their preferred metal. They'll do anything to get it.

— SHINTO YASAMOTO, AUTHOR OF
DRAGON HUNTING WITHOUT DYING

THE PASSAGEWAY HAD LED DEEP INTO THE MOUNTAIN, sloping steeply in places. Smaller passageways opened off to the side every thirty strides or so from which wary eyes peered at them. Other than the light crystals and lanterns mounted in deeply recessed alcoves, the passage lacked any illumination what-so-ever, only smooth granite mottled with veins of quartz and flint. Goru had led her down it in silence after the entire crew had disappeared in the blackness. At the end of the passage stood a massive pair of wooden doors that would not have looked out of place on the frontier. They still smelled of pine. Wooden shavings and sawdust carpeted the floor in front of them.

A smaller, human-sized door was inset into the right side of the dragon door. It was just as plain and held closed by a simple lever latch. To Yaz'noth, the entire construction probably had as much strength and integrity as a gauzy curtain. Ishe pondered what would lie beyond that door.

Dragons hoarded metals and ores of all types, even if a particular dragon preferred a single mineral for sustenance. The histories told in the Golden Hills claimed the conflict with Yaz'noth had started when the city stopped exporting iron and switched to the paper traded a small quantity of steel. Yaz'noth, a canny survivor of the Great Wyrm's Empire, had been preying on these shipments, making it look like the work of human pirates. With his food source gone, he abandoned the subterfuge and left a few crews alive to carry his message back to the Steward: "Tithe me cold iron or fall to my blockade."

The phrase "a tithe of iron" had been a curse in Golden Hills ever since.

Given that history and Yaz'noth's age, Ishe expected the dragon's personal chamber to be filled with gold and artifacts. She had steeled herself against gaping at an incalculable wealth. After all, she had spent a large portion of her childhood among the nobles at the Steward's palace. The paper trade brought wealth of all types.

But she had not prepared herself for the books.

Once that door opened, the potent cocktail of book musk and the brimstone-flavored dragon scent made a dizzying combination. Yaz'noth curled in the center of the chamber on a sparse bed of silver coins with the occasional fleck of gold. If he were standing on all fours, his antlers would scrape against the ceiling. The chamber was double the diameter of the bed. Crowding the walls were countless numbers of books stacked on twelve-high shelves that precariously hugged the sloping walls. Even from a nation that exported paper and maintained a vast library, at a glance, this collection outstripped the Steward's. All that paper in a room with a being that breathed fire and had blood the consistency of molten metal. Yaki would be scandalized.

Between the books and the apparently slumbering dragon lay a smattering of equipment and people. Placed near where his head tucked against his rump, a large table sat with a book on it. A series of lenses the size of dinner platters was suspended above it by the means of a steel scaffolding. A girl, no more than ten, sat on a stool beside the table, swinging her legs and reading a much smaller book. She wore a simple blue robe. Other magnifiers had other things beneath them: scrolls, a thin sheep with its chest cut open, and tools.

Everyone in the room sported at least one pip, except the little girl. The largest cluster of them stood around a metal cot of sorts. They shifted uneasily as Ishe's eyes fell on them. Goru gave her a slight push toward them and shut the door behind her. Yaz'noth's eye cracked open as Ishe made it halfway to the group.

"Gooood timing." The dragon's voice slurred. His golden eyes had dulled and a silver froth had gathered in the corners of his mouth.

Ishe stopped. The cot, which had a large crystal attached to the headboard, red like fresh blood, had no one in it. "Where is she?"

The dragon rumbled, his eyes rolling backward in his head. "I am stitching her chest back together now."

The words didn't make sense to Ishe, who blinked. "What?"

"It is called surgery. A healing discipline that mankind knew before Coyote ate the moon. It's more precise than medical crystals. It is…" Yaz'noth's eyes closed. "Almost got

89

it... There!" The dragon's body sagged seemingly in relief. "A pursuit of mine."

"W-why would a dragon learn to heal?" Ishe asked.

A tired chuckle filled the cavern. "Humans are fragile and offer a certain challenge that working metal does not. Now, would you like to see her?"

"Yes!" Ishe stepped forward as a twinge of fear ran down her spine.

"Word of warning. She probably will not thank you for this." With that, he lifted his head and spat Yaki's naked body into the cot. She lay there for a moment, just long enough to take a breath, and began to scream.

The throng of people burst into motion. A swarm of hands competed to catch flailing limbs. One foot caught a man right in the gut, and he went down. Ishe charged up to the bed and a woman smoothly moved out of the way. "Here! Take her hand. Tell her it's all right now." Ishe's hand caught Yaki's as it took a swipe at another woman. Her maddened sister crushed Ishe's hand with a desperate strength. Grimacing against the pain of the grip, Ishe folded the hand against her chest, hugging it as she sank to the edge the bed. "Yaki! Yaki, I'm here!" she shouted over Yaki's screams.

"Get it out! Get it out of me!" Yaki shouted as her struggles began to wane. "It's burning me!" The others were fixing leather straps to her limbs and across her chest.

"What did he do to her?" Ishe demanded of the woman with three pips at the head of the bed, her fingers stroking the medical crystal to life.

"It will pass. Hold on to her."

Yaki's eyes found Ishe's, wide with pain and madness. "It burns, Ishe! Get it out of me. Please!"

The light of the crystal danced on a meshwork of metal threads running through angry red flesh along her breastbone. Hands grabbed her cheeks and tipped a vial of something vicious and milky down Yaki's throat. She coughed and swallowed as the brightness in her eyes began to fade.

"What was—" Ishe started.

"Poppy milk," the woman said. "She needs sleep. They both do."

Yaki stilled, her body falling slack. The women reached down and closed her eyes. Ishe waited until she assured herself that Yaki's breathing had settled into a steady rise and fall before rounding on the dragon. "What did you do to my sister?!"

The corner of the dragon's muzzle twitched upwards in a bemused smile. "Exactly as you asked. I returned her to health."

Ishe stabbed a finger back at where Yaki lay. "Healthy people don't scream like that! They don't complain about a burning inside them! What did you do to her?"

"Hrrm, exactly? Would you even understand it? Your sister had a splinter lodged in her left ventricle. Extracting it tore a large hole in her heart. So, while both breathing and pumping your sister's blood, I had to construct a temporary replacement heart. It has been a most unique challenge. As for why she's screaming"—his head tilted side to side, uncertain—"well, she was conscious for almost the entirety of the process. It hurt and will continue to hurt until that crystal knits her ribs back together."

"You replaced her heart?" Ishe covered her open mouth and stared. "But that—"

"Is difficult but not impossible. Pain is temporary. Take it from someone who knows," Yaz'noth said as a pair of men wheeled in a bin loaded with ore. His jaw yawned wide and the men began to shovel in the rock as fast as they could handle. Mouth open, lips immobile, Yaz'noth voice continued. "Unsmelted? I've had a very long several days, flying and working miracles, to come home to raw ore?"

One of the men fell to his knees, shaking, pressing hands together in supplication as the other redoubled his efforts. "I'm s-sorry, my lord! But we have run out of coal to heat the furnace and there are no more veins of it in the mountain."

Casually, Yaz'noth reached out a massive paw and crushed the man. The crackle of bones echoed as he ground the corpse into the floor. The man had no time to scream. Ishe's teeth ground together as the dragon chewed his rocky meal once and swallowed.

Cruelty had always been in Ishe's life. Madria's temper had been as legendary as her wit. She recognized the turning away and subtle shake of the heads of the people around her. "Was that really necessary?" a voice asked, and, belatedly, Ishe realized it was her own. "Sir," she added.

A single huff of amusement emanated from the dragon. "No. It was petty. But I can be petty with my hoard. It is the point of their punishment."

"Punishment? You're their captain. They serve under you." Ishe could feel silent eyes on her back, stares begging her shut up.

"Me? A mere captain?" The dragon snorted. "Oh, if only. Miss Cog, tell my guest what you are."

The woman who led the operation to hold Yaki down stepped forward, eyes downcast. "For the crimes of our ancestors, we are not people. We are Lord Yaz'noth's things to use and break as he sees fit." Her eyes peeked up at the dragon, a slight sparkle of defiance in them. "But the time of our service is reaching its end."

"So it is. So it has. Nine generations have labored for attempting to enslave me. The tenth will choose their own way." The statement took the tone of a mantra. All the adults in the cavern bowed their heads and touched their fists to their hearts. The little girl in blue did not look up from her book.

"What? Enslave a dragon? Why nine generations?" Was everyone in this mountain mad? That last one, at least, Ishe managed to keep to herself.

"I'm sure someone will tell you the pitiful history of my hoard. Nine sounded good at the time. Had I understood how fast you vermin breed, I would have demanded eighteen." Yaz'noth yawned and tucked his head back by his rump. "Attend your sister. I expect you to be more grateful next time we chat, Rhino."

Ishe's head swam. She still didn't understand what had been done to Yaki. Squaring her shoulders, she stepped forward, trying to think about how Mother would phrase the question. A hand seized her shoulder and proved too strong to dislodge with a shrug.

"Stop talking to him," Miss Cog hissed, "or he'll kill another. Maybe even you."

"But he hurt Yaki. He promised to heal her, but he broke her!" Ishe's fingers were curling into fists as that awful scream echoed back to her. The oddness of the dragon and his slaves had distracted the rage, but it came flowing back. Miss Cog stood tall among the other Dragonsworn, but the crown of her shaven head hovered right under Ishe's chin. It would be an easy thing to pick her up and hurl her right at Yaz'noth's head. In the confusion, she could grab Yaki from her bed and run.

Run where? a voice in her head chided her. It sounded a bit like Hawk with Mother's tender steel. *Then what about the crew?*

"Peace, sailor. You're tired. We have food and rest." Miss Cog said. "In time, there will be answers."

Ishe pulled the woman's hand from her shoulder before allowing herself to be led back through the door.

Chapter Eighteen

❦

Your dignity is worth enduring agony.

— MADAM MANA, HEADMISTRESS OF
THE SCHOOL OF THE CULTURED
LADY

KA-CHINK, KA-CHINK, KA-CHINK. THE CONSTANT NOISE OF
the thing inside Yaki's chest pounded the pleasant haze away.
Overhead, a large, dark red crystal pulsed. She had seen its
like before in the hospital, both on her bed and in her sister's
at various times in their life. Yet this one had cracks spidering
through its core. It would not last much longer. Had it been
anything else besides a healing crystal, it would have been
shattered and recycled into cannon shells.

She attempted to reach up and touch it, but her hand
encountered resistance. Still bound. Not by thousands of
tentacles but by a simple leather strap. Pulling, she gave a
grunt of effort, but the strap held fast. Nothing moved. Still

bound and helpless. The metallic hammering of her heart increased as she twisted in her bonds, trying to find a weak point. The coarse blanket scratched her skin as she twisted beneath it.

"Yaki, stop. I'm here." A hand closed on her arm. Yaki tried to recoil from the touch but her body had nowhere to go. "Yaki. Stop, please stop." Yaki did not want to stop even for Ishe. Snatches of memory drove spikes of dread through her mind. The cursed tree, the dragon, the terrible place of hurt. Ishe had been there, between all those things. She had been there before the terrible place where things reached inside her and forced her to live through the pain.

Now Ishe was here in a dark room. Pleading with her to relax and threatening her with poppy milk if she didn't.. No sign of Mother. Answers were coming and they would hurt. Yaki wanted it all to stop. She'd had enough hurting. She wanted to rest. Maybe forever. So, she tried to shrink back from Ishe's touch and listen only to the *ka-chink* of her heart.

"Yaki! Yaki! Listen to me. It's all right. Please calm down. No one's going to hurt you." Ishe's words wormed their way over the mechanical pounding in her chest. "Come on back to me, sis. I need you to come back."

The only thing not secured was her head, so Yaki turned it away. Beyond her bed, a wall of rock greeted her. Not home. Neither the palace nor *Fox Fire*. Closing her eyes, she waited for Ishe to give up and go away. Yet Ishe's hand clung tightly to her own, callused palm pressing against her smooth one. Yaki pressed her lips together, trying to contain the question that she didn't want to know the answer to, trying to bar it in with anger.

It slipped out anyway. "Where's Mom?"

"Gone," Ishe said.

Tears came then as Yaki felt her world being pulled out from beneath her. Her metal heart stuttered, *ka-ka-ka-chink*, as she pitched into a yawning abyss of grief. The first hiccupping sob racked her body.

Echoing sobs came from her sister.

"You ox!" Yaki cried as Ishe worked to undo the restraints. "You couldn't sugarcoat that at all!"

"Mother wasn't one you could sugarcoat. She was always bitter." Ishe's hands thrust beneath Yaki's back and lifted. Yaki found herself pulled up into her sister's embrace. Any self-control she had left fled. Yaki bawled like a baby. The sound echoed off the undecorated walls and stung her ears. Mother was dead and with her went the perfect poise of the Flower. Without Mother, there wouldn't be a marriage or children or noble titles. Those tasks for which she had been honed and had taken pleasure in were falling away.

She cried until she ran out of tears, sobbing out every last drop pent up during finishing school and afterward. Through it all, Ishe's arms remained locked around her, unyielding and determined. At least that had not changed.

Finally, after Yaki felt emptied of everything, Ishe let her fall back into the bed.

"I'm going to get you some water," she said, wiping her eyes with the back of her hand and snuffling wetly.

In the brief moment she found herself alone, Yaki looked down at herself and the crisscrossed stitches that shone in the dull light. So much for all that hard work keeping herself unblemished. Broad pain still radiated with each harsh heartbeat. *The pain means you're alive, my Flower. You have to live with it.* Mother's voice echoed out of the past. Something pressed against the Death Panther's mark at that thought. "No," she said to the empty room, "I haven't forgotten you."

Ishe returned with a tiny woman bearing a tray laden with food and drink. "I don't think she's ready for all that," Ishe said.

"Then you will be surprised," the elderly woman snapped

back at her. She wore a brown woolen coat that went down to her ankles, probably to make up for the fact that she had no hair. As she entered the doorway, she paused to frown at Yaki. "Are you lucid?"

Yaki blinked. "That bedside manner is almost worse than my sister's."

The woman smiled. "Do you want this food or not?"

"Who are you and where am I—we?" Yaki asked as the woman tottered forward and placed the metal tray down in front of her. The tray sat on the rails of the bed, guided there by grooves. On it were a steaming bowl of stew, a bowl of brown rice, and a pitcher of water.

"Questions afterward. Eat now." The woman stepped back.

Yaki felt no stirring of appetite as she surveyed the tray, but picked up the decorated spoon. Its handle was formed from two long dragons twisting together. She studied it briefly. Something you'd see in a noble house that wanted to subtly insult its guests? It was far too fancy for a hospital, anyway. Twirling the spoon artfully as a matter of habit, she dipped the spoon into the oily stew and fished out a twisted chunk of meat. Smiling pleasantly, she shoved it past her lips, expecting her injured body to reject the offering. To her surprise, she swallowed without chewing.

"Good, yes?" The woman's smile broke into a grin.

"I don't know yet," Yaki answered truthfully; she hadn't tasted it at all. Her spoon was already retrieving more. She managed to chew the next piece, but the taste barely registered as something shifted in her head. One thought unified her entire being: FOOD! Food in her stomach, right now! The spoon became irrelevant; Yaki sank her fingers into the thick gravy and mashed the meat into her mouth. If a chunk was too big to swallow immediately, she'd pluck it out of her mouth to tear it in half with fingers and teeth. Rice was gulped down as if it were a liquid. Only once every trace of the meat and rice had been licked away did she turn to the pitcher of water. Which she drank like a thirsty spirit inhaled sake. Escaped water dribbled over under her chin and flowed between her beasts.

"More," Yaki gasped as she took the pitcher away from her lips. The sensation in her gut went way past hunger. She needed more food like her lungs needed air; a brand-new pain to go with her sprawling list. "More," she repeated, her gaze shifting to her sister, who stood with a hand over her mouth to cover her horrified expression. Not caring one whit, Yaki thrust her bowl out at her sister. "I need more food."

"You get any more and that stomach of yours will burst like an air bladder." The old woman sniffed.

Yaki focused on her. How dare she tell her what she could not do! To deny her—

"If your stomach bursts, we'll have to put you back in to fix it." She brandished a warning finger.

Yaki flinched as she remembered that place of torture and pain. An animal hiss rattled up her throat.

"Don't want that, do you? So, you'll stay in that bed until the bulge in your belly goes down. Then you'll get another round and only if you mind your manners."

The concepts of *later* and *enough food* spread through Yaki's mind like thick molasses. Yes, she was full now. And so tired. Looking down, she found a clear bulge in her belly. *A tithe of iron,* she thought to herself; *that would really hurt if I was wearing my corset.* Yaki eased herself back onto the pillow, a smile creeping onto her lips as she realized that for the first time in days, the agony had subsided. Her burning chest had toned itself down to a dull ache and exhaustion flowed into her bones, carrying her away. She sank into its tide eagerly, before memories of Mother could find her again.

Chapter Nineteen

In the Great Wyrm's Empire, each city in the Seven Saved Lands housed and fed at least twenty adult dragons. Is it any wonder that the Golden Hills imports its metals?

> — HON NISHAMURA, CHIEF
> HISTORIAN OF THE STEWARD'S
> ARCHIVES

"WHAT IN THE NINE HELLS WAS THAT?" ISHE HISSED AT the elderly nurse, Madam Ye. She had seized the older woman by the lapels of her coat and lifted her bodily into the air.

Madam Ye hadn't even had the decency to look surprised or even uncomfortable as she hung there. She stared back with a leer. "Heff. Your sister is doing very well. She listened to reason and went to sleep. Now put me down! Or I shall show you what a thumping is."

"That's not Yaki. That's an animal." Ishe jabbed a finger

back toward the room and resisted the urge to shake the infuriating grin from the woman's face. "What did he do to her in there? Why won't you tell me?"

"Ha! We're all animals underneath. You go without food for three days and then endure intense pain on top of it, and we'll see how civilized you are. She is doing fine, compared to the others," Madam Ye said.

Taking a long breath to think, Ishe could not find a hole in the woman's argument, at least not one big enough to justify slamming her into the wall. She set the woman down. "I want to see the crew," Ishe said.

Madam Ye smoothed the lapels of her brown jacket. "Have ta ask the Master for that privilege."

"Then let's go." Ishe stared down at the woman, but she remained frustratingly un-intimidated.

Madam Ye pointed to her shoulder, where one pip was worn. "You think I lived this long by barging in on the Master? Heh heh heh. You gotta speak to Cog for that."

"And where is she?" Ishe clenched her fists.

"Girl, you hide that temper when you go see him. As hot as you burn, he'll burn you back tenfold. Or worse, he'll go cold and cruel. Poor Tao was meant as a message for you, no doubt." Her eyes twinkled, hard and dark. "You might be a big bug to him, but you're still a bug. You'll make a bigger mess when he steps on you."

Ishe's anger flickered; she would be a bug to no one, not even a dragon. These people were pathetic, crawling around in tunnels and feeding on the scraps their armor-plated master deigned to toss them. The memory of that hapless miner pressed into a bloody smear rose unbidden in her mind. Still, fuming directly at Yaz'noth would be counterproductive. Crossing her arms, she snorted. "Fine. I'll be polite."

"You be polite with Miss Cog. You be grateful with the Master. That medical crystal is on its last legs. Could shatter at any moment, and it's the only one of that size we have." A wince must have shown on Ishe's face, because the little woman's cruel smirk turned into a tight smile. "You'll stew and ponder how to address a god properly. I'll send Miss Cog to fetch you after I'm good and ready." She paused and waited.

Ishe sucked in her breath. "Sorry for picking you up," she managed to force out.

"Not quite as dumb as you look." Madam Ye made a shooing gesture of dismissal.

Ishe turned away, heading back toward the bunkroom she shared with half a dozen other women. While Yaki's room was private, there were several larger rooms that housed injured Dragonsworn nearby. Mining accidents were apparently common enough to keep a staff of healers busy. Of what Ishe had seen, Yaki's bed was the only one with a sizable healing crystal. Other than that, she'd been shown a kitchen that always smelled of goat meat, and a cafeteria. A chair in Yaki's room had been her place of rest last night after Miss Cog had taken her to a hot spring to bathe. That had been a small moment of luxury.

Afterward, she'd been given a black woolen jacket that had been hastily tailored to fit her large frame and a skirt of the same material. Thankfully, the issued undergarments had been linen instead of itchy wool. Although she had laughed at the tiny frilly thing they called a bra. Apparently, while all the Dragonsworn wore the same brown jackets, what they wore beneath was self-determined. Ishe had the blushing woman who issued her the clothing fetch her a long bandage and bound her breasts, as had been her custom since the moment she stepped out of finishing school. Ishe always found the compression reassuring and calming.

Miss Cog and Madam Ye let her lie on her bunk and wait for hours. All the other women in the bunkroom were out working or making a point to be asleep. The woman with three talons appeared in the entryway, pushing aside the thick blanket that made a modest attempt to keep the bunkroom a bit warmer than the chilly passages. "Are you ready to see the Lord?" she asked.

Ishe was on her feet before she remembered not to act too eager. "Yes, I am." Her hand twitched with a suppressed salute.

"And what will you do first? Before you make a request?" Miss Cog's tone made Ishe flash back to the finishing school and the many times she stood in front of a black-dress-wearing matron enduring lectures on proper behavior.

"Thank him for saving my sister." Miss Cog's stance remained unchanged, so Ishe added, "Profusely."

Miss Cog gave a businesslike nod nodded, apparently satisfied. "Follow me, then."

Dragons were everywhere you walked in the tunnels: on plates that hung on the walls, over the doors that opened to countless rooms, and on tiles that adorned the floor of the wider passages. From each Ishe had a vague sense of unease. So many of the dragons sported Yaz'noth's sweeping antlers. How precisely did he keep these people from plotting against him?

Still, the path that Miss Cog led her through to the grand halls that preluded Yaz'noth's chamber had begun to adhere to her brain. *Three grinning dragon plates, take a left, a right after the door with a doorknocker fashioned like one of Yaz'noth's horns. When you see tiles of flying dragons on the ceiling, look for a nearly hidden ladder. And from the grand lair, a straight shot to the airship dock.* Unfortunately, hijacking one of the Dragonsworn airships would be out of the question. The dragon would retake the ships with ease. They'd have to work their way down the mountain and seek succor with the tribes in the valleys. But she'd need Hawk and Sparrow for that.

Such was Ishe's plotting mind when a boom of a voice split her thoughts in twain. "Ishe!" Yaz'noth spoke before her foot had crossed the threshold. "Oh, I had been hoping you would venture back to my lair soon. And without my even summoning you! What a glorious day."

Ishe froze as the dragon's grin filled her vision; his great eyes aglow with excitement. In his now-gleaming teeth, she saw her own wide eyes staring back at her.

A sharp elbow in her ribs jarred her thoughts off the circular track they had been stuck on. She had a job to do for now. "Ah, yes. I have to thank you for what you've done for me and my sister, L—" Her throat choked a bit, but she spat out the word anyway. "Lord Yaz'noth." She grunted as Miss Cog prodded again. "And I apologize for my rudeness yesterday.

The grin broadened even further. "Do not worry yourself on that note. All of us had our own ordeals yesterday. Come in and tell me how your sister is faring. I take it she's still alive. I've never made a heart before." Yaz'noth's head pulled back from the doorway, allowing Ishe and Miss Cog to enter.

"She woke up ravenous beyond reason, ate like a wild animal, and fell asleep again," Ishe said, barely keeping her tone cheerful.

He laughed. "All expected."

"She understood words after she had eaten, too," Miss Cog said.

"Oh, did she, now? Oh ho ho." The tip of the dragon's tail began to twitch back and forth, causing a group of Dragonsworn who were sorting through a pile of silverware near it to slowly back away from their task. "The daughters of the Silver Fox are made of tougher stuff than my servants."

"Well, sir—" Miss Cog began.

"Yes, Yes. Starving you all two decades ago was very

shortsighted of me. I have not forgotten Miss Cog. I'm a much gentler despot now. Wouldn't you agree?" he said.

Miss Cog nodded in reply.

"You starved your own servants?" Ishe asked.

"Not entirely on purpose." The head wobbled back and forth. "More neglect on my part. Much of the human food is traded for from the tribes that lay below the mountain and with the city-states. I'd been copying the designs on human flatware for centuries, and it gets tiring. I spiced up the designs." He chuckled. "Sadly, my beautiful visage did not enhance their market value. But it worked out in the end. The Dragonsworn use some of my finest designs today."

Ishe blinked. Then wandered over to the pile of silverware and picked up a fork. Unlike all the other designs in the caverns, she recognized this one. The swirls and eddies of the handle matched a set at the Palace. She had dined with them.

"In the time of the Empire of the Wyrm, several dragons were tasked with outfitting favored humans with weapons and armor. Infused with specialized crystals, they could do ridiculous things. Like a sword that cut the wind." The dragon smirked.

Ishe stopped toying with the fork. "This is crystal-infused silverware?"

"HA!" The laugh nearly blew Ishe off her feet. "I'm answering your question, 'What did you do to my sister?' Pay attention."

"So, they made those weapons, like my mother's sword, in what you call your forge?" Ishe looked from the fork to the dragon.

"Precisely." Yaz'noth nearly purred with pride. "Imagine me attempting to use a blacksmith's hammer with these." He waved a taloned forepaw over Ishe's head, and she had to shield her eyes against the coins that rained down from its underside. "This mountain is very rich in iron and silver. I eat the iron, and with the silver, I make trade goods to keep my little hoard alive. Without me, they'd starve. Dealing with humans is all about interlocking incentives. Carrot and stick. Which brings us back to your situation, dear Rhino." The dragon's grin turned sly.

"I will get you your quicksilver," Ishe said, adding to herself, *if I can't think of another way to get Yaki out of here. The crew, too.* "As soon as Yaki is on her feet again, we'll go together."

"Oh, that is such a pretty story. Sisters, hand in hand, going to betray the nation that birthed them. I've read one like that. It didn't end well, but that was half the fun." The dragon chuckled, his eyes growing distant for a moment before refocusing on Ishe. "Alas, we don't have time for that. A ship will be here to take you to the Golden Hills in two days."

Ishe could feel the rug about to be pulled out from under her. "Well, maybe she'll be well enough to—"

"Did I mention that it is the first heart I've ever made? All things considered, it's holding up very well, but a mechanical heart is hardly a long-term solution. And under the stress of a covert operation? Oh, we'd be lucky if it holds for two weeks. A month or two of peace and quiet under the mountain"—the dragon made a cutting gesture with his front paw—"max."

"But you said that—"

"Peace! Have hope, Miss Ishe. I am not planning on a betrayal. I keep my deals." He signaled to a group of Dragonsworn who had been loitering around a device that appeared to be a large fishbowl mounted on a conical base. They very carefully wheeled it over to Ishe. There in the middle of the bowl, suspended in a yellowish fluid and mounted between two slender medical crystals, a piece of meat pulsed.

"No. Is that—" Ishe stared at it. Extending her hand to touch the glass. It radiated heat. The fluid swirled around the thing.

"It is indeed your sister's heart. Note the hole on its side," Yaz'noth said.

Ishe shifted sideways, seeing a large gash in the tissue as the heart pumped, churning the occasional bubble.

"Those medical crystals are keeping it alive, but we'll need a bigger one to seal the hole. We can use the one that's currently keeping your sister together once she's finished with it. But if you manage to pick up a few on your errand, the process will be faster." The dragon rolled onto his side and stretched out his hind limbs, tapping his claws on the rock and generally looking smug as Ishe stared up at him. Her mind looked for an out but couldn't find any. She could feel the dragon's plan closing around her as surely as if she were standing on his tongue.

"I'll need my crew to come with me" was the only thing Ishe could think to say.

"Pick two. Preferably ones that are refusing to work, but it's no matter," the dragon said.

Chapter Twenty

It is only through the love of the Steward a houseless mongrel can rise so high.

> — MADAM MANA, HEADMISTRESS OF
> THE SCHOOL OF THE LADY, SPEAKING
> OF ADMIRAL MADRIA IN LETTERS

"NO. I WON'T DO IT, ISHE. I'LL KILL MYSELF BEFORE I go through that again," Yaki whispered into her sister's ear. She felt Ishe's grip on her hand grow from comforting to that of a vise, and the space between them filled with the sound of grinding teeth.

"You can't do that, Yaki!" Ishe glanced over her shoulder at the open doorway behind her.

"Why not? You have no idea what it was like to have your organs twisted out of you when you can't even scream. I'll choose death by a sudden heart attack any day. I won't let him do that to me. I'll tear open my wrist with my teeth if I have to." Yaki kept her voice steady, but her heart had begun to beat with fury. *Ka-chink, ka-chink!* She kept waiting for Ishe to comment on the sound.

"No!" Ishe nearly shouted before chewing on her lip in a conscious effort to restrain herself. Both girls' eyes flicked toward the door. No one appeared, but Yaki imagined one of the nurses hovering just beyond the doorway. "You can't simply give up. I worked too hard to keep you alive," Ishe whispered.

Wrapping her free hand behind Ishe's thick neck, Yaki pulled her sister's ear to her chest. The tender flesh screamed at the touch, but the pain barely registered compared to the memories of that terrible chamber flashing through her mind. "Listen," she hissed. "You hear that? You hear the machine he put inside me?" Ishe flinched in her grip, but Yaki managed to hang on for a few sharp heartbeats before a strong hand shoved her away.

Ishe shivered with revulsion as she spun away, hugging herself.

"I'm dead, Ishe," Yaki whispered. "I died the moment I hit that tree. That dragon's killed both Mother and me. Don't let him get you, too. Take Hawk and Sparrow and don't look back."

Ishe spun, red-faced. "You're not dead!" she roared. "You're alive!"

Yaki, surprised, shrank away from her sister.

"So, you got one little part of you that's ugly and makes a funny noise. Stop acting like your masts are snapped," Ishe hissed.

An incoherent noise of anger burbled up Yaki's throat; her hand lashed out against Ishe's set jaw. Ishe didn't even have the decency to flinch. "I'm not going to let that monster rip me open again. Nobody will do that to me again! Ever! I'll rip this thing out of my chest with my bare hands if I have to!"

"Stop being so dramatic! It's just pain, Yaki. We're both the children of Madria. We can endure pain." Ishe's eyes were cold.

It wasn't simply pain! Yaki wanted to scream at her sister. To grab her and shake her until she understood how she could still feel those tentacles in her chest, forcing her to breathe, to live when the only thing she had wanted was to die. Even healing now, every beat of her mechanical heart reminded her of that need denied. Her body no longer wanted to end, but to willingly subject herself to that? No, never again. Not for Ishe. Not even if it could bring Mother back.

The sisters bared their teeth at each other. Yaki swallowed, searching her mind for terms that her sister would understand. "Ishe, if you put me back there, I won't come out. I'll shatter."

Ishe's lips twisted into a snarl. "We don't have time for you to be a delicate Fl—" She coughed suddenly, spitting as if something horrible had crawled down her throat. "You can't act like Mama wanted you to act anymore. We're pirates, Yaki. We hurt people and take their money. That's the path Mother set us on when she slapped the Steward. And she knew it, too. You think she'd flinch from a little surgery?"

What would Mother do? Yaki pondered the question as she stared her sister down. Madria had danced the line between callous and caring. Her love might have been unconditional, but disappointing her always resulted in pain. Ironically, from what Ishe had told her about Yaz'noth, the pair might have gotten along rather well. But in this situation, with her freedom at stake, the Silver Fox would never allow herself to be chained like this. "Mother would cut her losses and leave her sister behind."

"Good thing I'm not Mom, then." Ishe turned and Yaki's blood ran cold when she saw the look in Ishe's eyes. A certain set of the jaw, an icy shine made her brown eyes nearly amber, like a wolf. Mother had the same look when she decided on a path of action.

"Ishe, I'm not going to let him flay me open like a fish again. Nothing you can do will change that." Yaki found herself panting beneath Ishe's stare.

Ishe's head shook minutely. "Fine." She spat the word. A step and she was back at the railing of Yaki's bed. "I leave in two days and you're coming with me."

Confusion flittered through Yaki. "What would be the point of that? This will just give out," she said, tapping the angry red flesh between her breasts.

A conspiratorial smile spread over Ishe's face as she reached around Yaki's shoulder to press her fingers on the raised scar in the shape of a paw. "Maybe Yaz'noth isn't as responsible for your health as he thinks."

"That was just to get me out that fucking tree, Ishe. So I wouldn't die alone," Yaki said. She couldn't hold the intensity of Ishe's eyes and looked down at her hands as she remembered the Death Panther's words.

"And that's it? Really?" Ishe asked.

Yaki did not raise her eyes. "That's it." The words tasted of a lie, although she couldn't put her finger on why. The panther had given her two gifts. If it followed the traditions in Sparrow's stories, then she could expect three more before the spirit would be done with her.

Ishe gave her a pat on the back. "I'll think of something then. Rest up." With that, the Rhino left.

Yaki sighed and fell back into the bed. Her stomach rumbled ominously. Maybe this time, she'd have the self-control to use the spoon, but she doubted it. The mannerly Flower was certainly dead.

Chapter Twenty-One

A dragon's preferred metal is set in the egg. All dragon hatchlings can subsist on other metals and stone if they have to, but their growth is severely stunted.

> — SHINTO YASAMOTO, AUTHOR OF
> DRAGON HUNTING WITHOUT DYING,
> ON WHY DRAGONS NO LONGER RULE

NINE GENERATIONS. THOSE TWO WORDS ECHOED through Ishe's brain as Miss Cog led her down through the mountain. A central shaft had been dug out through the middle, probably by Yaz'noth himself. Around the edge, a metal stairway had been constructed. It creaked and rattled with every step. Yet it held up to the footsteps of four dozen sailors. In the center of the shaft, two chains dangled, each link as thick as Ishe's arm. On one, baskets laden with ore and rock ascended. Empties rode down on the opposite chain. Archways branched off at regular intervals into the rock, yawning mouths of blackness.

A dread crept over Ishe with every step. There was little time before she'd be sent to steal several tons of quicksilver from a city that had exiled her family. There were a few allies who would shelter her, but none would tolerate actually betraying the city. Yaz'noth's errand would be doomed from the start. Try as she might to stay focused on her surroundings, she replayed the destruction of *Fox Fire* over and over in her mind. The way Mother had held herself when Ishe walked onto the command deck. How she leaned on Hawk for support. She had known what would happen as soon as that dragon appeared. The mistake had to have been when *Fox Fire* left the Golden Hills, laden with the bounty of quicksilver. Madria had beelined directly for Lyndon, betting that *Fox Fire* flew faster than any dragon. A wager she had lost. Yet it seemed like far too simple of a mistake for the Silver Fox to make.

The scaffolding bucked beneath Ishe's foot. Shocked from her thoughts, she cried out, stumbling backward and arms pinwheeling until her fingers caught the railing. Around her, the scaffolding roared with a chorus of groans. Ishe braced for the lurching sensation of gravity taking hold but only heard a quiet chuckle from Miss Cog.

"Do not worry, Miss Ishe. It will take much more than that to fell the Master's engineering. Dozens of those pulses take place every day." There was a certain glee in her eyes as Ishe picked herself up.

"I don't get it," Ishe said suddenly, her curiosity getting the better of her. "Why are you people still here? If you've made all these tunnels, you can tunnel out the side of the mountain and leave. It's not like he can come down here and punish you."

"Who would we be without him?" Miss Cog asked in return.

"I don't know. Join the surrounding tribes? If you're south of the Golden Hills, the forest will be thick with them. And they'll take outsiders. Just look at Sparrow."

"And be subjected to their gods? Who can stare into your mind and enforce their wills?"

Ishe cocked her head. None of the stories Sparrow told sounded anything like that unless an area was populated by the common villains, such as the Whirling Rock people. She had assumed they were metaphorical, but from the deck of *Fox Fire* she had spied a flock of rocks and seen places where lightning made love . The farther you got from the city-states, the more reality and metaphorical myth intertwined. "Tribes up north are not so bad."

Miss Cog shook her head. "The tribes build nothing to last for their children other than trinkets and talk of honor. They think of us as mountain dwarves. Here, we carve stone and walk among what our ancestors labored to build for us."

"And that's worth being slaves? For him to kill you when he's tired?" Ishe asked.

"He forced our ancestors to sell themselves to him." Miss Cog's smile reminded Ishe of her Master's. "But they did not do so for free. That bill comes due very soon."

"Your children are really free? That's not just something he says?" Ishe thought of the young girl in blue who had been in Yaz'noth's chamber when she first arrived.

"He honors his word in my grandchildren. On their sixteenth, they may present the Lord with terms for their service." Miss Cog's eyes shone with pride. "Or they can sail out into the world on their own."

This struck Ishe as deeply stupid. If word of this place got out, navies from multiple city-states would pound the mountain into rubble. Even a full-scale war between two city-states would be left off like an unfinished board game. There was one thing all the nations would agree on: the rise of a second Dragon Empire would be very bad for humanity.

"It's very lucky for your crewmates that our lord has relaxed the ban on outsiders. We usually do not leave witnesses, but we need to bolster our numbers," Miss Cog said after another set of steps. She pointed downward. Following her finger, Ishe saw below them a platform of sorts. A ring of metal ten feet wide that narrowed the shaft. The archway that perched on its edge shone with the light of fresh glow crystals. A team of Dragonsworn had positioned a cart on the very edge of the platform. Then, with the sharp ring of a bell, seemingly under its own power, it tilted up, spilling its contents down into the shaft below.

The men hurried back through the opening. But as they got closer, Ishe realized that the platform was not entirely unoccupied. Besides the entryway to the mine, an alcove had been dug, and a silver dragon lay curled there. Ishe had wondered where Yaz'noth's children had gone.

Miss Cog pulled a small metal disk from a pocket as they approached. It lifted its head to regard them with blue eyes that emitted their own light. Smaller than both of the young dragons that had attacked *Fox Fire*, this one was thin and lean. Only the top half of his body sported scales that shone. The rest of him was a muddy brown, with scales that were more crocodilian and rectangular than the overlapping metal plates on his back. Oddly, the dragon didn't have any wings.

"And why are you out here, Smooge?" Miss Cog's voice lilted up an octave.

The dragon hung its head like a scolded child. "Smooge bad."

"Were you fighting with Onion again?" Miss Cog asked.
"Nooo."

Miss Cog's voice went a tad sterner. "Did you bite your driver?"

"Noooo."

"Then what happened?"

"Nidge started it." The dragon mumbled. Unlike Yaz'noth, Smooge moved his mouth when he spoke, his lips shaping the words. He stretched his neck out, placing his snout very deliberately on the toe of Miss Cog's boot. His glowing eyes mimicked what dogs had mastered for millennia.

"Then why is Smooge out here?" Miss Cog made an attempt to look cross, but the smirk made her amusement obvious.

"Smooge finished it." His tail gave a little wag.

"Ah, I see. Will Smooge be good for me?" She opened her hand to display the metal disc. Ishe recognized it as a half of a metal coaster from *Fox Fire*.

It disappeared down the dragon's gullet before Ishe opened her mouth to protest. "Yes. Yum! Smooge be good."

Miss Cog ran a hand down Smooge's neck and scratched at the border between the silver and brown scales. Smooge stood and offered a taloned paw, his wrist encircled by an iron band joined to a thick chain by means of a pin. The chain curled around the dragon and into the wall.

"Couldn't he eat that chain?" Ishe asked, unable to contain herself any longer.

"No!" The dragon's head snapped in Ishe's direction, voice full of affront. "Smooge is good boy! Never eat chain. Never even think about it." A pause. "Taste bad, anyway."

"Easy there; she doesn't know Smooge." Miss Cog separated the chain from the anklet and patted the dragon affectionately.

Smooge's eyes narrowed as he looked Ishe up and down. "Blackcoat. Why blackcoat not in cage?"

"This one works. Blackcoats are allowed to work if they're good. What does Smooge do with blackcoats?" Miss Cog took a tone that anyone who attended a school when they were young would recognize.

"Smooge no listen to Blackcoats." The dragon walked behind Miss Cog, eyeing Ishe with suspicion. His legs were shockingly long and his shoulder about level with the top of Ishe's head. His overall body shape approximated a stretched-out pony, but his movements were those of a serpent, sinuous and graceful.

"Now let's go inside, and I'm sure you will be on your best behavior." Miss Cog's eyes met Ishe's for a brief moment.

Crossing her arms and rolling her eyes, Ishe feigned nonchalance at the woman and her dragon child. Questions bit at her brain. The slaves of a dragon raised his children with tenderness and care? They willfully endured nine generations of abuse for something? But she pushed that all aside. She had less than two days to figure out how to smuggle Yaki out of the mountain. Nothing else mattered.

Chapter Twenty-Two

✿✿✿

Taking on a spirit's chimerage is sacred. As the spirit has honored you, you must honor them. The tie between cannot be hidden from those who look for it. To conceal a chimerage is inviting the blessings to become curses.

— SEEK FIRE, CHIEF OF THE TURTLE
CLAN OF THE LOW RIVERS TRIBE,
LOREKEEPER

As Yaki licked the last bit of gravy from her fingertips, she became aware of two pairs of eyes watching her from the doorway. One pair was big and brown, belonging to the girl in a bright blue kimono. The other, tiny blue eyes, was set in the head of a white kitten clutched in her arms.

Self-consciously, Yaki took the previously untouched hot towel and wiped the saliva from her fingers. Giving the girl a pleasant smile, she picked up her spoon. This had not been the first onlooker. Dozens of eyes had fluttered through the open doorway. The girl was merely the first she had not heard coming in time to feign sleep. *Let her look,* Yaki thought with some bitterness. She'd been reduced to an infant: eating, sleeping, and shitting in the pot in the corner while listening to her life clang away in her chest. Picking up the bowl of steaming rice, she began to shovel the grains into her mouth, swallowing it down without chewing. A painful howl radiated up her torso, demanding more, faster, but Yaki tightened her grip on the spoon and defied it. It could wait. A few more seconds would not make a difference. Naked and alone, watched by a curious child, the need for dignity outweighed the ravenous stomach.

The bowl emptied. Yaki scraped her spoon across the shiny white glaze, but no new grains popped into existence. No more food. Her stomach churned, direly insulted. Yaki closed her eyes and gripped the railing of her bed, waiting for the stomach to realize it had food, for the sensation to pass.

"Why are you so strong?" a voice, which could only be the girl's, asked.

Opening her eyes, Yaki discovered that the girl with her cat had taken a bold step inside the room. Placing her age proved difficult. Baby fat rounded her cheeks, but the curves of the kimono hinted at hips and breasts. Yaki judged her no more than fourteen years, but given the inherent smallness of the Dragonsworn, she couldn't be sure.

Yaki plastered a serene smile on her face. "Are you supposed to be here, child?"

The girl's chin took on a stubborn angle. "I am of the tenth generation. I go where I wish. And I ask any question."

"Do you get answers to all your questions?" Yaki countered as she tried to remember what Ishe had said about these people and their dragon king.

"Mostly. Except for Lord Yaz'noth. He points me at

books." The kitten struggled to escape as she took a wary step closer. "You don't have books."

"Well, I don't understand what you mean by *strong*. I'm still bedridden." Yaki glanced at the door, willing the specter of Madam Ye to appear and save her from this strange interrogation. The hunger had begun to grudgingly subside, and in its wake, exhaustion would come. Eat, sleep, and shit.

The girl shook her head. "You're doing better than all the others! Unbound, eating with a spoon! No vomit!"

"What do you mean, *others*?" Yaki said, her eyes narrowing at the girl. "The dr— Your lord had never made a heart before. What happened to the others?"

The whispered scrape of soft pads on rock filled the silence as something unseen in the room shifted. The kitten hissed. Surprised, the girl's grip opened enough for the fluffy thing to twist away. It ran out of the room with a tiny yowl of fear. "Princess!" he girl called after her pet, and took a few steps toward the door. Pausing a moment, she spun on her heel and flung herself back at Yaki's bed. "Please! I can't say anything more. I'd break my promise, and as the oldest of the Tenth, I will not do that."

Yaki looked down and saw the desperation in those young eyes. "Why?"

"Because I am the oldest of the Tenth and it will be my turn someday." She looked up through the railing, gripping it white-knuckled like the bars of the cage.

There were so many explanations Yaki could give. She had lived in the fresh air and sunshine. Her mother's mixed blood. She had endured a childhood of disciplined training. All of that had given her body the strength to survive this torture.

"Does the oldest of the Tenth have a name?" Ishe asked. "And what do you mean, it will be your turn someday?"

"Mei," the girl responded. "And I can't tell you that. Not yet."

Yaki huffed in frustration but then considered. Knowing certainly wouldn't make the girl's life easier. Pulling herself up into a sitting position, Yaki twisted to display her mark to the girl, wishing that she could see it herself. "You see that? Do you know what that is?"

"A paw?"

"A promise. Have you ever been outside this mountain, Mei?" Yaki turned back and pulled the blanket up over her shoulders.

"I've gone with the traders to see the wild people in the valley," Mei said.

"Don't call them that," Ishe snapped. "If you want to know what this mark means, then you'll have to ask them, and you won't get far if you call them that. Learn their proper name. After I was wounded, I knew how to call for help. Knew what to offer." Yaki looked down at her hands. Were they less delicate than before? The formerly manicured fingernails were certainly gone. One had been torn off, the rest broken and nibbled. Did she eat like a beast because of the iron heart in her breast, or because the Death Panther had taken Flower instead of Yaki of Madria?

"It's a mark of the wild gods, isn't it? You're a servant of them." Mei stood up suddenly. "Are you a spy?" she hissed, stepping back.

Yaki chuckled and grinned at the girl. "I'm a pirate. Looking for riches to plunder. Sometimes, that makes for odd bedfellows."

"You can't be the first, then! Pirates are honor less and oath breakers. You can't be the first!" Mei turned and ran, leaving the sound of slippered feet pounding down the hall. Yaki stared at the empty doorway.

These people were proving themselves more insane by the

minute. Ishe was right. They had to get out of there. The Golden Hills had to be warned that they had an adult dragon so close to them. And what in the nine hells did he want the quicksilver for? As far as she knew, there had never been a quicksilver dragon.

Reaching over the side of her bed, Yaki undid a latch and swung the railing down and out of her way. Swinging her legs over the side of the bed, she paused a moment before hefting herself onto the pads of her feet. Her legs wobbled but held. The metallic clanging of her heart beat slow and steady.

The pain blossomed after two halting steps toward the doorway: a burning in her chest, a sizzling in her ears. A wracking cough seized her on the fifth step, and she spat to clear her mouth of the sudden, oily tang. The pain grew to the point that it felt like a bundle of hot coals had been trapped inside her, searing her insides as she reached the door. Breaths came in great gulps, never enough to quench the fire inside, and the air felt choked with smoke.

She retreated to the bed, and her lungs breathed in the magically fresh air. Or at least as fresh as the air down there got. The crystal banished the pain. "You know," Ishe gasped, "a little more strength wouldn't go amiss."

The Death Panther made no reply.

Chapter Twenty-Three

‌

After the death of her sister, the earth thrashed with fitful dreams. The Death Panther visited all who traversed the slopes of the Spine.

— SEEK FIRE, CHIEF OF THE TURTLE
CLAN OF THE LOW RIVERS TRIBE,
LOREKEEPER

MINING, ISHE DECIDED, MAKES AN AWFUL LOT OF ruckus. It was very different from the howling of the wind over a hull, sharper and far more painful. She did her best to ignore it. Behind her, dozens of men and woman scrabbled over the face of a stone wall. The largest carried drills nearly as long as she was tall, in teams of two or three. The others stood ready with shovels and pickaxes. The drill would bore a hole as wide as a fist, pack it with explosives, and then once the miner retreated a young dragon snaked his head around a safety barrier, squinting carefully. Then emitted a burst of fire. The wall splintered as the explosives went off with a dull thud. breathed fire until the powder exploded. Then the swarm descended on the crack, some pulling the rock free as others worked on shoring up the roof. Miss Cog assured Ishe that there was an order to the chaos, but Ishe simply saw undisciplined mobbery.

Now she sat with her back to that process and facing the crew in what Miss Cog called the learning confinement: a wide cage with a bench in it. Twenty crew members were crowded on that bench, watching her with suspicion. They all wore the same black coats that she did, marking them as "guests." The trouble was that Ishe stood outside the cage and they were in it. None of them looked happy to see her.

Hawk sat in the middle of the bench, her towering bulk taking up the space of two men. Her back was straight and uncowed. Sparrow sat several people away, hunched and miserable, occasionally coughing into the back of his hand.

"You didn't escape?" Hawk scowled down at her.

"No, and they have Yaki, too," Ishe said.

Sparrow and several other crewmates looked up sharply at that. All who did bore the same grid-like tattoos on their faces. All were members of the Low Rivers Tribe.

Hawk's face remained impassive. "She lives?"

Ishe could not help herself from shooting a side-eye glance at Miss Cog, who stood stubbornly beside her. "She lives. The lord of the mountain is tending her injuries and making me beholden to him." Ishe's cheeks began to burn with shame. She had been the daughter of an untouchable legend, and now she was consorting with a dragon who had an unsubtle dagger to the throat of her sister. "I've... I've been tasked with returning the quicksilver we lifted. I'm allowed two companions." She raised her eyes to Hawk and then to Sparrow. Hawk held her gaze, face impassive but somehow channeling deep disappointment into Ishe's soul. Sparrow looked away and coughed.

"You are not my captain, girl. You cannot order me to do this," Hawk said.

The word *girl* sliced through Ishe. She had been the third mate on *Fox Fire*. Now she was just a girl? Had that really been all she was to Hawk? Hadn't she proven herself a little?

"Hawk." Sparrow voiced a gentle reproach to his wife, then stood, giving Ishe a weak smile. He opened his mouth to speak.

"Sit down, Sparrow," Hawk said like the whisper of a sword easing from its sheath.

Sparrow closed his mouth with a wince and sat back down with a muttered "Yes, my love" in the Low Rivers tongue.

Ishe licked her lips. "I'm not commanding, Hawk. I'm asking. I need your help." Some invincible Rhino she was. Each eyeball on her made her skin burn and itch.

The silence was only broken by Sparrow's muffled coughing. Hawk's left eyelid fluttered with each one. Everyone on the ship knew that Sparrow's lungs could barely handle a day or two in a city. Down here among the rock dust and stagnant air? Ishe didn't know how long he'd last, but it would be miserable every moment.

All of her fellow Low Rivers crewmembers watched Ishe as well, faces stony. One man stood and faced Hawk and started talking in their language too fast for Ishe to follow. She caught the words *abandonment, Headwoman,* and *coward.*

"Hawk, we can fi—" Sparrow began.

"No options. We'll go." Many of the other crew stared down at their knees; a few more stared at the big woman in open disgust. One stood simply so he could turn his back on her.

Ishe bowed her head. "Thank you."

Sparrow looked as if he wanted to turn into his namesake and fly down a very deep hole.

Hawk stood, grabbed two of the narrow bars of the cage, and wrenched them wide. As she stepped through them, Miss Cog scrambled backward, letting loose a shrill whistle.

Men with crossbows swarmed from cavern openings, but by the time any of them had pointed their weapons, Hawk had swept Ishe up into a great bear hug, crushing the girl to her ample chest. Ishe's feet dangled a foot from the ground. "Understand that I hate you now. I'd rather hate you right now than my husband," Hawk said, and squeezed until Ishe felt something pop in her chest.

"I understand," Ishe wheezed, blinking back tears of pain.

The pressure eased enough for Ishe to take in a breath. "I could not save Madria," Hawk said. "She trusted the trickster and he led her to her doom. If that is your path, do not expect anyone to follow you."

The hug relaxed a fraction more, still tight but not painful. "Do not follow your mother's track," Hawk whispered again. Then Ishe became aware of a thick finger prodding her in the ribs. Two light pokes, followed by two long ones. Lantern code for the letter F.

"Tap it tonight. Alone," Hawk whispered in Low Rivers out the side of her mouth. "Return it."

Ishe's arms were pinned to her side, but she managed to return the pattern into Hawk's rock-hard stomach.

Immediately, Hawk dropped Ishe and held her arms up in the most nonthreatening manner possible for a nearly eight-foot-tall woman. Ishe counted four heavy crossbows and a smaller one held by Miss Cog, all trained on Hawk. Grinning maliciously, Hawk stepped back into the cage and bent the bars into place.

Miss Cog lowered her weapon and it disappeared into a pocket of her coat. "What is she?" she demanded.

Ishe shrugged. "She's Hawk. She's always been that way. Word of advice, don't piss her off." That elicited a few hollow chuckles from the crew, and Ishe began to walk back to the entrance of the cavern. There was nothing more to do there.

Should Miss Cog try to pry into Hawk's history, Ishe had more than enough tales to share. Hawk stories were a common pastime among the crew whenever the first mate had been safely out of earshot. Some of the stories might even be true.

Chapter Twenty-Four

Many a fool has attempted to raise a dragon from its egg. While cute, they make up for it with the tendency to breathe fire at anything bigger than them, and the ability to chew through a granite wall in an afternoon. All such stories end with either the escape of the dragon or the death of the handler.

— SHINTO YASAMOTO, AUTHOR OF
DRAGON HUNTING WITHOUT DYING

THE DRAGONSWORN SEEMED PERFECTLY CONTENT TO leave Ishe alone with her thoughts. Only Madam Ye and Miss Cog conversed at all. The others limited themselves to monosyllabic answers. Yet in order to do what Hawk asked, she needed not the privacy of thought but actual privacy. That was rare. While the Dragonsworn made a show of leaving her to her own devices, someone always lurked nearby. Still, there wasn't much to do other than wander about the hospital caverns. The bunkroom she shared with the nurses always had someone in it, and without the sun, time ebbed and flowed oddly.

She'd guessed there were at least five hundred people living in the mountain and manning ships, but it was impossible to tell. If there had been a mine behind each of those passageways, then the mountain itself could house thousands. The traffic through the tunnels was sparse, though. Groups of people traveling in two or three were encountered, but rarely more than that. The only exception was the shift change for the nursing and kitchen crews. During that time, the echo of their voices filled the caves. The conversation would sullenly die away as soon as someone noticed Ishe.

Occasionally, she'd catch flashes of the blue kimonos of the Tenth, but they hurriedly exited the room before Ishe could ask them any questions.

Internally, she snarled with frustration. Yaki was supposed to be the sneaky one. All Rhino wanted to do was bust heads and bend bars like Hawk. Now she had to ditch a tail without him or her realizing they'd been ditched, then find a place alone. Had Sparrow somehow smuggled Blinky into the mountain? Or had he tamed some new critter? Maybe Hawk had made contact with the mountain itself?

Then she remembered Goru, the Dragonsworn who had delivered her to Yaz'noth. The thought promptly caused her to lose interest in the small bowl of stew she had been eating. Goru had said he had a private room and left nothing to the imagination of what he wanted to use it for. The idea made her skin crawl, and her mind flashed back to her horrible finishing school. She gave it an hour to think of a better solution but came up with no alternatives. So, she caught the arm of one of the nurses in the dorm and asked. The woman's thin eyebrows nearly rose off her head, but she flagged down one of the blue children, a thin girl who couldn't be more than seven. The nurse attempted to make the girl promise not to talk to Ishe, but the girl simply took Ishe by the hand and led her off into the tunnels, seemingly deaf to the scolding of the nurse.

"So," the girl began once they were out of the hospital warren. "You were a pirate. With a ship?"

"Privateer," Ishe answered somewhat warily. "We only attacked shipping from rival states." *Unless a Golden Hills captain had specifically pissed Mama off,* Ishe added to herself.

The girl shrugged disinterestedly at her explanation. "Did you have cannons? That launched crystal charges?"

"Yes, why?" Ishe examined the girl closer and saw in the dim crystal light that her blue kimono had soot stains around the knees. The girl ignored her question and began to pepper Ishe with detailed inquiries into the operation of ship-borne crystal cannons. She knew a bewildering number of details of their assembly, but not their use. How do you fire it, account for wind, what do the different charges interact with? Finally, Ishe had to snap, "I don't know!" and the girl fell into a grump.

They walked in silence for a bit. Ishe could hear the soft footfalls of her ever-present shadow, always out of sight.

"I know someone who does know," Ishe offered.

The girl stopped. "Who?"

Ishe smirked. "I'll need a favor first."

"I see." The girl walked in silence for a moment, and Ishe suddenly got the impression she was much older than she looked.

"Look. Goru offered me privacy for a cost I'd rather not pay. I need a place to hide for an hour. My mother is dead. I need some time alone. All alone. Then I don't have to go to Goru's at all," Ishe said.

"Oh!" the girl said brightly, "You need a crying cave. I

know all about those. I went there a lot when my mama died." She paused. "This person, is she nice?" she asked.

"He'll be bit grumpy about being in chains, but that's your problem," Ishe offered.

The girl scooted closer, whispering conspiratorially, "I want another favor too."

"And what would that be?" Ishe asked.

"I'll let you know." She glanced over her shoulder in the direction of Ishe's shadow and grabbed the cuff of her jacket. "Now follow me." She took three more loud steps before she veered suddenly down a darkened tunnel.

Ishe stumbled after her into the blackness. The rough rock wall bit her knuckles as the passage narrowed to the point she had to turn sideways. "Come on, come on!" the girl urged as she pulled Ishe back into a lit tunnel, her eyes glittering with mischief.

After several more twists and turns, the kid stopped at another fork in the rock. Unlike most of the passages that had clearly been carved out in some manner, this portion had the look of a natural cave. Stalactites hung from the ceiling, and the broken stumps of stalagmites tried to catch the toe of her boots.

"Here we are." The child tugged her forward, and in a few feet, the passage opened into a cavern lit with a huge glow crystal. Nested among the spiky rocks and walls were dozens of roughly oval stones, each the size of Ishe's head. "Don't worry; they don't hatch…usually. It's my crying place."

"Are these—"

"Yup, this is a dragon clutch. You gotta have at least two talons of trust to be in here. Your shadow is trying to earn her first." She smiled. "Okay, which one of the blackcoats is this gunner?"

"Koshue. He's the one with the long beard braid. He's an

expert gunner. The best on *Fox Fire*," Yaki said, watching the eggs for any sign of movement.

"Yesss!" The girl's grin flashed brighter than any crystal in the cave and sprinted off.

Ishe hoped to the gods that she hadn't just screwed Koshue over as she listened to the girl's footsteps die away. Still, setting Koshue up for some minor annoyance beat being forced to bed any man, in Ishe's book. If they got out of this, she'd make it up to him.

Picking up a rock, she began to beat the pattern Hawk had given her against the stone.

Chapter Twenty-Five

❧

Never doubt that the All-Father has a sense of humor.

— SEEK FIRE, CHIEF OF THE TURTLE
CLAN OF THE LOW RIVERS TRIBE ON
WHERE THE SPIDERS CAME FROM

BLINKY DID NOT LIKE THIS SHIP. IT DID NOT HAVE enough kittens. Blinky had only found one so far. There were flying-squeaking-things down in the holds, but they were not as tender as cats. Skinny-human-thing had told Blinky to hide, so Blinky did. Skinny-human always helped Blinky.

Hiding was boring. Easy to hide when human-things never look up. And when they did catch him, he simply scuttled off before they looked again. Blinky missed home. Missed feeling the purr of home in his legs. The noises here were sharp, loud things that interrupted his sleep and made him chitter irritably. Nothing regular. Deeper in the ship, the walls sang with the harsh sound of cracking stone.

He missed a lot of other things as he sat in his little spun nest near where the squeaky-things lived. Missed sneaking up into the laps of the sisters for affection. Missed the steady diet of rats. They tasted better than the squeaky-flying-things.

Tap, Tap… Tap… Tap.

Blinky froze and almost let the squeaky-thing he held in his front legs flutter away.

The pattern repeated and Blinky rubbed his pedipalps together with joy. Skinny-human's call! Blinky skittered side to side. A Fetching! Blinky loved fetching. Where did he put the fetching thing? He felt through the dark in the pile below his nest; mostly eaten squeaky-things. He hoped Skinny-human would come and clean out the nest soon.

There! His leg tasted the flavor of web he used for fetching and pulled it from the pile. Then he skittered after the sweet rhythm pulsing through the rock. Skinny-human-thing must have moved. Tapping was not so deep as the sharp rock-breaking place. Blinky zipped through unfamiliar tunnels, following the sound, leaving a thin thread line behind him to mark where he had been. The number of human-things increased with the light of the tunnels, but Blinky was in a hurry, and the rock shook with the sound of a scream or two in his wake. The rock tasted wet as he got closer to the source, and he could not help himself from chittering in excitement.

Chapter Twenty-Six

Never let them see you cry; it's undignified. Do it in the next room over, loud enough for everyone to hear in the pauses of their conversations.

— MADAM MANA, HEADMISTRESS OF
THE SCHOOL OF THE CULTURED
LADY

ISHE WAS ABOUT TO GIVE UP AND MAYBE CRY FOR REAL when she heard a sound that could only be produced by an eight-legged nuisance. "Blinky?" she asked.

In answer, the monstrous shape of the ship spider scuttled into the cavern, zipped down the wall, and pounced on her with a high-pitched *scree* of joy. Eight legs hugged her as Ishe staggered from the impact of the fifty-pound spider. Rapid-fire spider kisses, the flicking of the long sides of Blinky's two-inch fangs, impacted Ishe's shoulders and neck. They tickled until the skin went numb. Ishe managed to get an arm free of the eight-legged embrace to scratch at the seam between his head and body. The spider churred happily and slowly lowered himself to the ground.

Now a few steps away, Blinky's larger eyes were looking her up and down. Ishe noticed he put no weight on one of his legs and had something small grasped in its claw. "What have you got there, Blinky?" Ishe held out her hand to the spider. He scuttled back and forth a bit, indecisively. She flexed her fingers. "Come on, give it to me." He dropped the small ball of webbing into her palm.

"Good Blinky! Very good spider." Ishe lowered her voice several octaves like Sparrow did when he praised the creature.

Blinky clicked happily as Ishe began to pick at the ball of webbing. She had no crystal knife to cut the spider silk, and therefore it had to be unwound. Fortunately, Blinky had not used sticky webbing, and she found the loose thread end after a minute or so. The spider's many eyes seemed to twinkle with laughter as she unraveled several feet of webbing to reveal a tightly rolled scrap of paper.

Sparrow's tight script greeted her eyes as she unrolled the paper: *We have found two ways out. Ventilation shafts drilled into the side of the mountain. Too small to fit now. Second. Main door at bottom of shaft. Guarded, but not by many.*

The other side of the paper was blank. A place to write her own response? If only she had brought a pencil. They had two choices. Either a massive uprising and fight for the main gate, or the four of them sneaking out a side shaft, if she could find an Earth charge to widen the way. A Sparrow plan and a Hawk plan, if Ishe had to guess.

In the Golden Hills, there were medical crystals three times the size of the one that hung over Yaki's bed. If Ishe could trade the knowledge of this place for one of those, Yaki might be able to live with the metal heart indefinitely. Her original one might grow back too. Screw Yaz'noth and his experiments.

Ishe thought about storming the gate and dismissed it. Hawk would be able to take it, but the melee would certainly reach Yaz'noth before it was over. Escaping through the ventilation shaft might give them the head start needed to reach the forest below and disappear into it before Yaz'noth took to the skies to look for them.

All she had to do was find a cannon charge or ten.

Ishe briefly searched for something that would serve as a pencil but found nothing. With a grimace, she slit open a finger with the small metal kitchen knife she had taken and wrote *I will find a charge* in blood on the back of the strip. Once it was dry, she rolled it up and handed the paper back to the spider. "Bring this back to Sparrow."

Blinky blinked all eight eyes at her.

"Uh... Hide?"

"Fetch?" asked Ishe.

The spider chittered and snatched the paper from her fingers before scuttling off into the darkness.

Ishe let out a breath. Next step: remembering those awful lessons on crying.

Chapter Twenty-Seven

❧

In the Dragon Empire, humans directly serving a reptile were assigned rankings in talons. Rankings were from one to four. Five talons meant they were personal servants of the Great Wyrm himself.

> — HON NISHAMURA, CHIEF
> HISTORIAN OF THE STEWARD'S
> ARCHIVES

IT WASN'T HARD TO FIND HER WAY BACK TO THE quarried tunnels, but Ishe's sense of direction failed to guide her to the hospital warren. Instead, she found herself heading downward, deeper into the mountain. After doubling back utterly failed, she barreled on, hoping to run into someone, anyone who could guide her back to the passages she knew.

The heavy clang of machinery answered her hopes as the tunnel began to widen. A laugh echoed down the hallway. Ishe dug her fingernails into the webbing of her hand and focused on the pain. It hurt, but her eyes remained clear. She thought of the blue ball of fire that had consumed her mother. Nothing. Those tears had been spent. Her thoughts shifted to Yaki and the pain in her eyes. Her look of utter desperation still cut to Ishe's core. A sniffle started. That had been her fault. Only the Rhino was to blame for this. And only Ishe could get them out of there.

Holding those thoughts, Ishe called out, "Hey!" She walked in the direction of the voices. Turning the corner, she found three tan-coated Dragonsworn, two men and a woman, staring at her in open shock. "S-sorry," Ishe began. "I've gotten lost from the hospital wing. Could you show me the passage back?"

One of the men, a head taller than the others with a thick gray beard, crossed his arms and scowled at her. "Where is your escort, Blackcoat?"

Ishe sniffed, wiped her nose with the back of her sleeve, and stuck out her chin. "I have parole."

"Left him in the dust, did you?" The second man laughed. "There is no escaping from the Lord, girl." His voice had the crackle of advancing age, but his hairless face showed only crow's feet in the corners of his eyes. "Eight generations of us have tried. Tunneled through the rock, stormed the gates, stowed away on the ship. All found by man or Lord."

The woman had a pregnant belly that pushed her coat out. She was far younger than the other two, still with traces of baby fat in her round cheeks. "You are the pirate bitch's daughter, then? The uninjured one?" Her eyes were hard and flinty.

"I am the daughter of Madria, the Silver Fox. And I'd be wary of putting on airs when you serve a dragon," Ishe said before her brain got ahold of her angry tongue.

The eyes of all three glittered dangerously in the dim crystal glow. The big one spoke first. "Madria was nothing to our Lord. So are you until you prove yourself and earn a coat of a different color."

Ishe's head rocked back a fraction in confusion. These people were slaves to a dragon. Why on earth would she want to join their ranks?

The laughing man stepped forward with a distinct limp. "Come with me. I will guide you back to your minders before these two make you swallow your boot."

"You sure, Kori? She is a big one," the big man warned.

Kori waved him off. "If I don't come back in an hour, raise it with the Lord. I had a talon once. He might even remember me." He offered his hand to Ishe and she took it. He immediately clasped her forearm to his side, forcing her to bear a portion of his weight. "Come along now. Miss Ishe, isn't it?" She nodded and allowed herself to be led away from the other two.

"Better watch your tongue, miss. The Eighth and Ninth are a mite prickly about their position," he chided once they were out of earshot. "Too focused on gaining favors from the Lord so he might favor their progeny of the Tenth."

"So, you're a Seventh?"

"Sixth! One of the few left." He grinned. "Is it true? Your sister is well?"

"She is surviving so far; I'm not sure I'd call it *well*. Without that crystal holding her together, she'd be in a lot of pain. Why?" Ishe looked at Kori. The old man stared straight ahead, eyes fixed on something that Ishe could not see.

"But she's getting better?" The old man's grip tightened.

"Yes. Her body is healing." Ishe said, fighting down a sudden urge to check on Yaki. It felt like it had been too long since she checked.

"Hell of a thing. He is actually getting better at it. Most don't make it this far. It's about time."

"What usually happens when he replaces something?" Ishe asked the old man.

"Anything the Lord manufactures runs hot. Simple things, a bone or joint, they'll heal eventually, but they hurt. You can see it on their faces. They might make it a year; one made it two."

"And then?"

"It breaks. Snaps, shatters like glass. They start coughing up blood, and in a few hours, they die. 'Great honor,' my foot. I gave up my talon as soon as I realized my leg wasn't going to straighten out ever again. 'Cause you know he'd try to fix it." He gave a wheezing chuckle.

"And the not-simple things? What happens when he replaces something like a heart?" Ishe asked, dreading the answer.

"Heh. They eat. They sleep. And they scream. Then they die. But each one has lived longer. Everybody's sighing with relief that he found your sister. He's been hoping for a good mining accident for months now. With your sister no longer screaming, maybe he's finally figured it out. Maybe he's got a way to hang on to the Tenth after all. The grand bastard."

Ishe stopped. "Figured what out? What does my sister have to do with the Tenth?"

He patted her shoulder in a grandfatherly way. "If I tell you that, I'll be a bloody smear on the stone tomorrow. The Lord always knows when you break an oath."

"What do you mean by that? Is that how he controls you all? Some sort of geas? Look, maybe I could help out the rest of your family if you could tell me some things." Ishe clasped the man's arm as if he were supporting her. "Please," she whispered.

"And give up seeing what happens in these few years?" He laughed. "No, girl. The ghosts in these passages have a horrible view of the happenings, and somebody's got to tell them about their descendants. I'm old, but I'm not wishing-for-death old. Have patience. The Lord himself will tell you soon." He smiled open-mouthed, displaying yellowed teeth with a few gaps. "Who knows; mayhaps you two are simply made of tougher stuff."

"We do come from a tough family," Ishe said, allowing the man to change the subject. In truth, she didn't have much idea what her lineage had been. Madria had had the look of the northern tribes, but her Low Rivers language was tentative at best. And who their father had been changed every time you asked Mother. Some whispered that they were the Steward's bastards, but Mother said the pair of them were born before Madria caught his eye. The old man nodded and said nothing more. Ishe didn't attempt to pursue the conversation. Her thoughts were turning over the next stage. She had done what Yaz'noth asked: selected two crew to accompany her. The next logical step would be to ask about other resources. When attempting to remove several objects from a building, things like explosives might be needed. Indeed, it might be best to find out what tools the dragon had to lend her.

She stopped and Kori looked at her quizzically. "Could you take me to Yaz'noth's lair instead? I need to speak with him."

"Or be talked at?" Kori's brow arched. "Let's turn around, then. It's back this way."

Chapter Twenty-Eight

The Ancients built in steel and poured stone. Over two thousand years later and we still build with paper and wood. Its a lucky decade when the majority of the city hasn't needed rebuilding.

— HON NISHAMURA, CHIEF
HISTORIAN OF THE STEWARD'S
ARCHIVES

"Gooood, you've selected!" Yaz'noth boomed as he looked up from the lenses of his reading table. "Not surprised you picked the big one. Too bad she's a package deal with this little Sparrow fellow."

Ishe's heart slammed against her chest, and she mentally tried to shove it back into place. These things were perfectly reasonable for him to know. Miss Cog had had plenty of time to inform him about Hawk and Sparrow. "Sparrow has plenty of talents that are useful. He's educated and can pose as a merchant with ease."

"And the facial tattoos won't raise any alarms?" Yaz'noth asked.

Ishe scoffed. "They'd hardly be the only ones in Golden Hills to bear those marks. The Low Rivers lands border the frontier, and merchants travel freely."

"I see," said the dragon, a ghost of a smile playing at the edge of his maw.

"Now that I have my crew, I need to see what I'll have to work with."

"Do you have a plan?" Yaz'noth tapped a single claw on the rock, and the Dragonsworn manning the magnifier turned the page of the book.

"Depends on the equipment I have. I can't exactly carry the quicksilver shoved in my pockets," Ishe said.

"Pretend you have whatever you need and tell me your plan." *Tap*. Page turned.

Ishe hoped the dragon wasn't actually paying attention, because she was making this up on the fly. "The Grand Foundry is located just inside the main walls." Ishe remembered the great dome-shaped building, belching out a plume of black smoke as *Fox Fire* set sail. "We cannot get an airship there. All airships except for the Steward's personal yacht are moored outside the city. We'll have to transport several tons of quicksilver outside the wall fast. The quickest way will be directly through."

Yaz'noth's head swung around to look at her directly. "And how do you plan not to get wiped out during, say, the hours it will take you to get out of range of the artillery cannons in the city by horse and air sledge?"

"Huh." Ishe thought hard. What would Mother have done? Other than planning something like this for months. "Most of the cannons are designed to take out ships, not ground targets. We'll need a distraction. Something like a dragon flying in from the west?"

"The whole point of me buying that quicksilver, and yes, I paid for it, was to not expose myself to risk and announce my existence to Golden Hills yet. Try again, but something that might work."

"A bigger explosion, then, on the opposite side of the city or at the palace," Ishe said.

"You seem to like making things go boom," Yaz'noth said with a wry chuckle. "Is this Sparrow an expert with crystalline charges?"

"I am," Ishe replied with confidence. "Mixing up elemental crystals for varied effects is something I've always done." She didn't mention that she usually only mixed charges for her hand cannon.

Yaz'noth snorted out twin clouds of steam. "I suppose if you could devise a plan that didn't involve knocking down walls, you wouldn't be called the Rhino. Very well. You there." Yaz'noth pointed at a hapless-looking fellow who was tinkering with some equipment. "Show Miss Ishe the armory. Mark what she needs and have it loaded as soon as *Scale* docks."

The man bowed deeply. "Yes, Master."

He hurried up to Ishe. "This way, please."

Ishe wondered how many charges they would need to widen a ventilation shaft.

Chapter Twenty-Nine

❧

The transformation of low-quality crystals from dangerous trash to ammunition turned the entire industry inside out in the unfortunate case of the "healing bomb" that was literal.

> — HON NISHAMURA, CHIEF
> HISTORIAN OF THE STEWARD'S
> ARCHIVES

ISHE DECIDED YAZ'NOTH MUST PREFER TO SLEEP IN cramped spaces, because the warehouse stood triple the size of his lair. The entire cap of the mountain had been hollowed out, reinforced with columns of stone, and braced with steel to hold the roof in place. The deep grooves in the floor gave her the impression that Yaz'noth had personally done the digging. Boxes and crates of all sizes stood on evenly spaced racks with clear labels that designated them as exports (mostly silver products) and imports (food and mining equipment). The shelves of imports were barren. If the warehouse represented the dragon's more-liquid wealth, then judging from the amount of empty shelving, he'd nearly bankrupted himself with the purchase of the quicksilver. Or perhaps with the ship coming in soon, the exports had already been brought to the dock?

The Dragonsworn leading her said nothing as they walked deeper into the warehouse. Beyond the shelving, things devolved into disorganized piles of random goods, tea sets, rugs, furniture, and knickknacks. Ishe recognized it all as what her mother called dross, the stuff from a ship raid that you take that looks valuable but you can't sell. Judging from the sheer amount of it, when Yaz'noth took a ship, the Dragonsworn stripped it bare. Ishe knew collectors in Golden Hills that might wet themselves in their eagerness to pick through the dross of three hundred years of pirate raids. The path they walked appeared to be a fairly recent addition; on either side of it, the piles of goods were larger.

At the end of the path, they came to a small fortress built of metal boxes bolted together. Two Dragonsworn guarded the entrance, each with a hand cannon at the ready. They straightened when Ishe's guide came into view. Ishe noted that each sported a single pip or talon on their shoulders and briefly put a fist to their hearts in salute. Their eyes on Ishe were not friendly.

The metal passage led to another gate and pair of guards. These opened another locked gate. Then they walked into a magazine. The secured chamber stood perhaps a hundred feet wide and deep, its ceiling stretching all the way up to the rock above. A man sat at a desk by the door, and thick logbooks were piled on its corner. Beyond him, against the sheer metal walls, were racks of elemental shells. Their bright copper canisters shone in the crystal light that emanated from a pole in the center of the room. On the other side of the room stood a collection of weapons. One half of them appeared to be a motley assortment of swords, axes, and the odd hand cannon. The others were more uniform: sets of swords, hand cannons, and defense shields, although the shields lacked any sort of crystal that would allow them to function. They were entirely metal, and Ishe recognized pieces from the batch that Yaz'noth had expelled to make room for Yaki.

From the size of the shells, the largest no bigger than the span of Ishe's hand, Ishe knew that the Dragonsworn had no trade with any nation's military and their contacts on the black market were few. All the shells fit cannons typically found on merchant ships, designed to dissuade stray young dragons and bottom-feeding pirates with tiny skyships rather than doing major damage. *Fox Fire* had used shells in its smallest cannons twice as big as the largest ones in this magazine. From the marking on the shells, the collection consisted of primarily Earth and Fire shells. That would suit Ishe's purposes fine.

The man at that desk finished scribbling something in his logbook and looked up. His eyes looked large in his thick glasses. "Why, hello, Captain Ronga," he addressed her guide. "It's been a long time."

"Ronga is all now, Tannis. I'm escorting Miss Ishe, a blackcoat, to see what she has to work with."

"It wasn't your fault; you will always be Captain to me. I will put this visit in the log. Look all you like, but I'll need the Master's signature to check anything out before *Scale* docks." He dipped his pen back in his inkwell and bent over to write. Four gold pips shone on his shoulder, even more than Miss Cog.

"It won't take long. There is nothing here that will take out a city wall." Ronga turned back to Ishe with a sort of victory in his eyes.

"You don't have any loose crystals?" Ishe asked.

"After the uprising of the Sixth, they were forbidden," Tannis said. "It was a pity. It slowed the miners down without them. The black powder we use now is horribly dangerous."

Ishe stepped forward and peered into the rows of shelves, looking at the manufacturing marks that adorned the side of each shell. "Hey, girl! Step away from there! Your little plan won't work. We do not have the shells you require," Ronga barked.

"That sounds more like you don't want me to succeed. What happens if I do manage to bring back that quicksilver? What does an iron dragon need with it?" Ishe continued to search the shells. They were of many different makes and types, and probably all acquired through piracy. No answers came from the two men as Ishe fell to hands and knees, searching. "Ah-ha!" She spotted a collection of forty shells that bore the symbol of a one-eyed wolf that marked the Grissom Brothers arms manufactory. Peeking back at the men, Ishe saw that Tannis had pulled a hand crossbow from somewhere and it was leveled at her back. Ronga simply glared daggers at her. She showed her hands. "Not touching, not yet. But you're very wrong about not having enough here to blow a hole in the wall."

Tannis's eyes narrowed. "We've attempted to harvest crystals from these canisters before. The attempts tend to yield more fingers than crystals."

"Then I have something to show to Yaz'noth," Yaki told them.

Chapter Thirty

An Earth shell as big as ones fist will blow a hole through an iron plate two inches thick. The same shell will barely chip an iron dragon's scale. And yet...

> — SHINTO YASAMOTO, AUTHOR OF
> DRAGON HUNTING WITHOUT DYING

YAZ'NOTH WAS INDEED INTERESTED TO LEARN THAT small civilian charges could be safely disassembled. He ordered all the Grissom Brothers charges be brought directly to his lair. A brief scuffle of authority occurred between Miss Cog and Ronga about who would retrieve the charges, but Miss Cog won the honor and Ronga was sent back to repairing equipment.

"Had you not destroyed *Fox Fire*, this would be unnecessary," Ishe said as they waited for the arrival of the charges. She had been provided with a small box to sit on. "We had plenty of military charges in the hold."

Ishe heard the dragon shift, a metallic groan as iron in his hide flexed. She refused to look up at him. Instead, she kept her eyes on the small kitchen knife, examining its blade and wondering if it was thin enough for the trick to work.

"I couldn't take that chance. If half the rumors were true about her and wild gods, then anything less than full atomization would be risky. Killing things is always trickier the second time around," Yaz'noth replied with amusement.

Ishe's knew she should bite her tongue and stop talking. "Mother was a ship captain, an admiral once. She had no time to be a sorceress, too."

The dragon chuckled. "That's not what her biography says. Did she not learn the name of the winds from the Cheète Tribe so the wind would always blow in her favor during the war with Valhalla? Is that not why she became an admiral in the first place? Even ships with propellers need favorable winds."

Risking a glance upward, Ishe was relieved to find the dragon's eyes not leering at her. Instead, the great neck reached past her as Yaz'noth focused his attention on a bookcase near the entrance. "If that were true, then you would have never caught us," Ishe said, remembering the foul smell of the winds on the deck of *Fox Fire*.

A brief sucking sound and his head pulled back. Something rectangular dropped from his lips. Ishe caught it on reflex. It was a book, bound in green leather and three fingers thick. Turning it, she read *Secrets of Admiral Madria Revealed* in neatly tooled characters. "You'll have to decide, then, if your mother's luck ran out or if mine is simply greater."

The door banged open. Ishe turned to see Miss Cog and several men hauling carts of shells behind her. "Showtime," Yaz'noth attempted to whisper as he pulled back to watch the proceedings. Dragons, Ishe observed, were terrible at whispering.

"These are all the shells that are marked with a one-eyed wolf, Master. Eighty-eight Fire, one hundred seventy-two Earth. Inventoried, they are actually the largest manufacturer. All obtained via raids, never purchased," Miss Cog reported as the three carts laden with shells were wheeled in front of the dragon.

Ishe swallowed. If ever Miss Cog wanted to kill Yaz'noth, setting off that much ammunition would be a good try. Even in individual casings, that much of it piled together might crack the mountain. Stepping forward, Ishe grabbed an Earth shell and prayed this would work. "As you know, most nations require civilian ammo be made to explode if tampered with. Ostensibly, this prevents pirates from getting their hands on too many elemental crystals. What a crystal grove does if they need a little cash boost is they make a few batches of ammo with defective safeties." Holding the brass casing up toward the dragon, she stuck the tip of her knife into the seam that held the propellant canister to the globe around the elementally charged crystals. Slowly, she worked the tip of the knife around the circumference until she felt something right below the surface. That would be the small Fire crystal that, if bent, would set off the entire charge. Noting where it was, Ishe set the charge down on the floor, holding it lightly so it did not roll. Everyone stepped back as she brought the heel of her knife down on the shell.

A small *crunch* was heard. A tiny wisp of smoke drifted from the seam.

The globe did not take off careening around the room, and she grinned. With a reinsertion and final twist of the blade, Ishe poured small green crystals on to the floor of the lair. Cubes tumbled a short distance away from her feet, like little six-sided dice.

"And that's how pirates away from safe ports get their ammunition," Ishe said. She was wondering how she could carry two to three shells' worth of Earth crystals when her black jacket had no pockets. "Grissom Brothers ammo can be made by a half a dozen groves. And you'll pay more for it. But it's worth the cost."

Ronga plucked a Fire shell from the cart and turned it over in his hands. "What bit are you smashing, girl?"

"The detonator crystal." Ishe smiled. "It's a bit of a knack, though. Generally, we do this right on the ship deck. If you do it wrong, the propellant goes off. On the deck of the ship, it usually goes overboard. In here"—Ishe glanced at the very flammable artifacts and books that lined the walls of the room—"be my guest." She offered him her knife, handle first.

"No," Yaz'noth said. "Miss Ishe will open all of them. Right here. In front of me."

"That will take me—" Ishe began.

"The better part of twenty-four hours. It will give you something to do instead of running away from your minders." The dragon eyes flashed with amusement. Ishe's shoulders wilted. He knew about her "private" time. She wasn't going to get any more.

"What about the ones I fail to disarm? I'll need a safe place to throw them. Particularly as my arm gets tired." Ishe's gut twisted. How much sleep would the dragon need? And was his vision keen enough to catch her slipping occasional crystals down her sleeve? How good was he at reading human expressions? If only Yaki was doing this instead of her. Yaki could lie so convincingly that even if you spotted a falsehood, you wanted to believe her anyway. Ishe had never mastered that art. Nor had she wanted to until she stood under the gaze of Yaz'noth's massive golden eyes.

"You will throw them into the safest place possible: down my throat. Try not to do it too often. Fire crystals give me horrible indigestion, a condition that sadly destroyed a large portion of the Third generation," Yaz'noth said with a horrible smirk. Nobody laughed. "Ronga will assist you in disposing of the live shells."

"My Lord?" Ishe could hear Ronga's nervous swallow.

"Yes. Should Miss Ishe mutter *oops* or some such, you with your well-rested arms will grab the shell and toss it down my gullet. Also, make sure she's not slipping highly explosive crystals down her pants. It wouldn't help anyone if she accidentally sets herself on fire." Yaz'noth's expression remained somber, but the tip of his tail curled and uncurled like a very amused cat. "You do want that third talon back, don't you, Ronga?"

"Y-y-yes, sir," Ronga stammered.

Miss Cog snorted with amusement while the thudding of Ishe's heart climbed up into her ears. Had he seen straight through her or was he simply naturally cautious? Even if she did get the crystals, she would still need time to find a way down to Sparrow and Hawk. *Patience,* she told herself, *wait for an opening.* "If I'm going to do them all in one go, I'll need some tools."

The dragon nodded. Ishe described what she needed, and after swallowing a few ingots of bronze, Yaz'noth heaved up a ball-shaped hammer, a tube to channel errant shells, and several bronze boxes to store the raw crystals. Ishe and Ronga were brought meals, stools, and a table to work at. Ishe piled twenty shells in easy arm's reach and placed the tube in front of her. Ronga helpfully bolted it to the table and then sat beside it, his back to Yaz'noth.

Ronga insisted on placing one of the vessels to Ishe's right, where he could watch her dump the crystals from the shells. Once everything was set up, Ishe began with zero fanfare. Finding the detonator with the knife, she placed the nose of the shell in the tube and whacked it with her hammer. The detonator fizzled and she worked the propellant canister off. She settled into a rhythm. On board *Fox Fire*, she had only done a few shells at a time to harvest ammo for her hand cannon. Now faced with a mountain of shells, the task resembled peeling potatoes, except these potatoes could explode if you didn't peel them just so.

Ronga's gaze was a heavy thing. His eyes were constantly on her hands, his face only betraying a slight tic as she brought the hammer down on a shell. The great dragon watched them with the stillness of stone, only the slight sulfuric breeze of his breath indicating that he was more than a statue, his head as motionless as the one that hung in the great hall back home.

On the thirty-third shell, she made her first mistake. The hammer came down slightly to the left of the spot. The propellant began to sizzle. Ishe cursed, pushed it into the tube, and dived away from the table. *BLAM!* The propellant went off. Yaz'noth's mouth opened just enough to admit the screaming projectile, while the half-full box of crystals flew off in the other direction, spraying needle-like Fire crystals into the air.

Nobody breathed as the crystals rained down. The empty box fell on its side and the clatter echoed through the lair. Ishe closed her eyes and focused on thinking very cool thoughts, waiting for the *whoosh*. This could be her moment. She gripped the front of her jacket in preparation to rip it off. If the crystals ignited and she managed to not become a human torch, she could run out in the panic with a few of the Earth shells.

There was no *whoosh*. Yaz'noth stood, his eyes closed as if in concentration. All the tiny crystals that littered the area had darkened to the color of clotted blood. As if they'd all been expended.

"Everyone in the rooms. Get brooms, sweep this up, and start again. Find a new place for that box," Yaz'noth said with the evenness of someone concentrating on something else very hard. Ammo crystals were supposed to be insensitive to crystal singing, but apparently, dragons played by different rules.

Shakily, Ishe got to her feet. Perhaps there were additional reasons Yaz'noth wanted this done in front of him.

Chapter Thirty-One

❧

Some classify beauty as a weapon. Note those men, for they are those who are open to being swayed by it.

— MADAM MANA, HEADMISTRESS OF
THE SCHOOL OF THE CULTURED
LADY

"*TSK!*" Madam Ye squinted down at Yaki, hands on her hips. "Back to bed with you, young miss!" Using the crook of her cane, she hooked one of Yaki's ankles and forcibly dragged her across the stone floor. As Yaki crossed the threshold into the room, she let out a gasp as her lungs suddenly remembered their function. A coughing fit immediately seized her and she spat bloody gobs of mucus onto the ground. "You silly, stubborn girl. Did I not tell you that the only thing keepin' you alive is that crystal? And that's going to be the case for a long time. I'll not have you follow my poor Wux and his leg. He pushed too hard, and not a week in the mines did it snap right off." The old woman snapped her fingers with a *crack* that echoed around the room. "Just like that, it did. Bled out like hitting a vein of lava."

"Where," Yaki panted, "is my sister?"

"I told ya. She's busy with the Master. Now you climb right back in that bed, young miss, or I'll haul you there by your ear." The woman delivered a hard kick to Yaki's buttock. The blow drew a fresh curse from Yaki, although more from surprise than actual pain.

"Get moving, girl. You got yourself out of that bed; get yourself back in it." The woman crossed her arms and scowled.

Grimacing, Yaki began to crawl back toward the bed, the fire trapped in her chest trying to burn a scream out of her. That had been the farthest she'd been able to get so far: five steps from the door. Too bad her legs had given out when she turned back toward the room. She'd lain there for who knew how long, feeling the smoke and flame in her chest slowly make it harder and harder to breathe. At least now screaming was an option again. The pain eased as she inched closer to the medical crystal. She hated it. It felt like a chain around her very spine. And now Ishe must have gone and done something stupid. It had been over a day since she'd seen her. What on earth could she be doing in this hole in the ground?

Yaki flopped into the bed like a dying fish and sighed as she enjoyed the sensation of an effortless breath.

"I see your bedside manner hasn't changed since the time I was a child," said a voice Yaki recognized. Miss Cog stood in the doorway.

"You weren't a spoiled pirate princess like this one. Wouldn't know gratitude if it kicked her in her pretty little face." Madam Ye glared at Yaki as two more women squeezed past Miss Cog. They went to the head and foot of the bed and started jostling it. "What do you think you're doing, Cog, girl? She'd got to eat in another hour. And while she's better eating, it still ain't a pretty sight."

"The Master wishes to see her now," Miss Cog stated.

Madam Ye said nothing and stood out of the way as Yaki was wheeled into the passages. Her protests were quickly swallowed by the clatter of her bed moving along the uneven stone floors. All she could do was hang on and try not to bite her tongue. She could barely hear the *ka-clank* of her heart over the ruckus her bed made.

Yaki counted twenty-seven glow crystals in the ceiling of the tunnels before she arrived in the lair. Her body started to tremble as soon as the sulfurous odor hit her nostrils. The memories seized hold of her then. The stink of that scent as things reached inside her body.

"No no no no no." The mantra tumbled from her lips as she saw the wall of dull metallic scales before her move. Things were speaking, but she didn't hear them. She had to get away. Great golden eyes swung toward her, mounted above a terrible maw filled with teeth the size of her arm. A hand roughly shoved her back into the bed as she tried to swing herself over the railing. So, Yaki did the only thing available to her: she pulled her thin woolen blanket over her head and cowered.

Someone laughed, deep and ugly. "What is this? Peekaboo? Miss Yaki, hiding is no way to greet the one who is currently saving your life."

"You hurt her. You hurt her very badly, Yaz'noth," Ishe's voice came.

A low rumble shook the floor. "Humans and pain. Why does it cripple your kind even after it has been removed? I will give her time, then. Keep working. You can have your break once she's willing to speak to me."

Yaki heard the creak of wooden furniture as her sister

sighed. A sharp *clink* sounded, followed by a sizzle. Shifting slightly, Yaki peered out from under the blanket to see her sister sitting at a table and emptying elemental shells. The dragon's great maw was no more than five feet away. Yet Ishe didn't seem to notice the hungry eyes on her. Her hammer would rise and fall, and then after a moment of fiddling, she poured green crystals into the bucket at her side. Ishe slumped slightly, the slope of her shoulders tired as she picked up the hammer again. Yaki felt her heavy metal heart slow.

There was no escape. Now even Ishe was working for the dragon. Yaki listened to the heart. *He isn't going to put me back,* she told herself.

Waiting for another shell to be finished, Yaki gathered her courage and then sat up. She held the thin blanket to her breasts and smiled shyly. "May I have some clothes, Sir Yaz'noth?"

A golden eye flicked in her direction, but he waited for Ishe to complete another shell before the great head floated toward her. "Does a doctor ask his patients to put on clothes before an examination? You may stop, Ishe."

Ishe slumped with a sigh and began to shake out her arm.

"Stand up. Let me see your wounds," the dragon commanded. Yaki did not move, clutching the blanket as if it were some sort of protection. A claw tip tapped against the stone floor. Ishe had turned in her chair now and gave Yaki a slight nod.

Yaki's pleasant expression faded to a scowl as the dragon displayed nothing but a quiet impatience. All activity in the room as had stopped, and Yaki felt every eye like a searing brand on her exposed skin.

"Can we at least have some privacy? Please? There are men here," Yaki asked with downcast eyes, focusing on past humiliations to fuel the fire in her cheeks. To show her body here, to everyone, would rob her of one her most potent weapons. Once people saw what was underneath, she could not hint to them of perfection that did not exist. "Please, sir."

The dragon laughed again, deep and mean. "No, but most of my Dragonsworn have jobs to do at the moment. Do they not?"

The sound of footsteps resumed in the cavern, but Yaki's skin still itched with the feeling of eyes. One of the attendants helpfully swung down a railing to allow her out of the bed. She hovered nearby, no doubt waiting for the command to haul her forcibly to her feet. Yaki played with the pros and cons of making them do that. Would willfulness gain respect? Or would submission massage the dragon's ego? Her body moved before her mind had fully decided, casting off the blanket and exposing the ugly strip of angry flesh that ran between her breasts. Silver wires crisscrossed it, straining to hold her together. She stretched out her arms to the sides to display herself for him. *Here I am, you bastard*, she thought.

Yaz'noth came so close that Yaki had to resist the urge to slap him. The cavernous nostrils threatened to pull her in as he gathered her scent with lungs that had to be larger than her mother's cabin. He got several strands of her long, unkempt hair, at least. "Definitely healing," he concluded after a long, ponderous moment. "You cannot stand to be out of the range of the medical crystal?"

"No. Not for longer than a few seconds," Yaki said, seeing no reason to lie.

"She's been testing the limits, my lord," Miss Cog said. "Trying to get to her sister on her own, I suspect. She is not an obedient patient for Ye."

At this point, Yaki's stomach let out a loud, wet growl. Snickering seemed to echo in the chamber. Yaki felt as if her face might ignite.

"Healthy appetite?" Yaz'noth asked.

"At this rate, she'll chew through two months of rations in a few more days. Feeding time in a half hour," Miss Cog said in a cold, clinical voice, looking at a clock on the wall. The urge to scream at them to stop talking about her as if she were a cow or something was building in her lungs, but Yaki managed to resist the impulse. A lady was always on display, but she hated this particular part of the role. Instead, she edged slowly toward the bed. No one objected when she slipped back beneath the blanket.

The dragon continued to interrogate Miss Cog as to Yaki's sleeping and eating habits. They were going to feed her here, she realized to her dread. *Everyone here would watch!*

As the two continued to converse, Ishe approached. Deep bags under her eyes indicated it had been a while since the Rhino had last slept. "Where have you been?" Yaki hissed as Ishe embraced her, the scratchy wool coat making her skin itch.

"Been around," Ishe said as one of those sleeves strayed down Yaki's back. "You should rest for a bit." Ishe pushed her back and Yaki felt a dozen or more sharp edges jab into her back, clustered around her lower spine and kidneys.

Yaki covered her grimace with a broad smile. "I was worried about you, sister. They wouldn't tell me anything."

"I had to prepare to return the quicksilver that Mother took." Ishe returned the false smile.

"Stole," Yaz'noth corrected, momentarily straying from his conversation with Miss Cog, which had drifted from Yaki to the subject of proper Golden Hills trade goods.

Ishe had taken Yaki's hand in both of hers and was pressing words into the palm in lantern code. *Need more, stay as long as you can.* "The ship will be here in less than a day, so I've had to hurry."

Nodding, Yaki wanted to slap Ishe. How in the nine hells did she expect this to work? With all the jostling on the way back, one of the crystals would be bound to leap out! She'd have to hide them, but where and how? Still, she slipped on a mask of a pleasant expression and said, "You look like you need some rest."

Ishe nodded. "I'll sleep on the ship, but I could do with some food."

"We'll have the kitchen send up a portion for both you and Ronga with Miss Yaki's meal," Yaz'noth said.

"I will make it so." Miss Cog bowed.

"In the meantime..." Yaz'noth said.

"Yes, sir," Ishe replied, and turned back to her workstation. The dragon smiled as he returned to his place to watch her work.

Yaki began to transfer the crystals from beneath her back to her pillowcase. The only trouble was that she didn't know where her second minder's eyes were. She stood behind the bed and to the left, so Yaki had to assume she was always being watched. She put on a show of drumming her nails on the metal railing. Her stomach joined in on the act, gurgling loudly as mealtime drew nearer. All the while, she palmed the crystals out from under her and shoved them into her pillow.

"Uncomfortable?" Yaz'noth asked after her stomach gave a particularly audible roar.

Yaki froze, still clutching die-shaped Earth crystals in her closed fist. "Merely ravenous," she said with a thin smile. The food was late and she still had two sharp crystals digging into her ass. Her awareness had been focused on the eyes of her captors, but now it snapped to the clock. Over fifteen minutes late.

Chapter Thirty-Two

Seed crystals, crystals so pure that they continually bud off new crystals, are rare treasures. Their worth, while imaginable, might stretch one's ability to spend.

— HON NISHAMURA, CHIEF
HISTORIAN OF THE STEWARD'S
ARCHIVES

WOULD IT BE ENOUGH? ISHE'S ENTIRE MIND WAS centered on that question. As she had hoped, Ronga's attention had begun to waver by the time she had finished with the Fire crystals, and she had positioned the Earth crystal box just out of Yaz'noth's field of vision. Neither appeared to notice that she wasn't completely emptying all the shells. Every four or so, she twisted her wrist a bit early, letting the last few crystals tumble down her sleeve. A quick stretch before the next hammer swing moved them down past the elbow, preventing their escape. She'd managed to dump a shell's worth into Yaki's bed. By the feel of it, she had another half to a quarter of a shell still cutting into her triceps. She hoped it simply felt that way. Dripping blood would lead to discovery.

Earth crystals alone merely exploded in a concussive blast when used in the air. That was useful for crowd control but not as good as a Thunder crystal. However, any nearby rock and metal flowed like water for a few seconds after each blast. An iron-sided warship did not fear Fire. It feared Earth shells that could open portals in its armor. A die-sized crystal could blow a hole the size of her finger through a half-inch steel plate. Against softer stone, it would be an order of magnitude more potent. Judging by Yaz'noth's desire to control the crystals, it was probably much more effective than the black powder the miners used. Too effective to trust them with.

Ishe risked taking a bit more from the next shell. Ronga's attention kept straying to Yaki as the burbling noise of her sister's bowels echoed. The clatter of people working in the lair had faded. After Yaz'noth apparently won his little contest of wills with Yaki, the Dragonsworn seemed to have lost interest. Only a cluster of blue-clad children had remained. Several had approached the bed but were stared down by Yaki's two minders. Neither women had said anything or acted as nurses. They stood and watched like practiced soldiers. It was they who most worried Ishe.

The door to the passages below opened with a creak, disturbing the rhythm of Ishe's thoughts and motions. She put down her hammer to see Miss Cog returning with a cart of food.

"You're late," Yaz'noth observed.

"Apologies, Master. The kitchen is having…spider trouble." Miss Cog said.

Oh, no, Blinky. What have you done now? Ishe thought.

165

"We cleaned out the cavern spiders over a hundred years ago. It didn't get one of the Tenth, did it?" Yaz'noth asked.

"No, sir. It made off with a goat haunch, no children. Although it might explain why some of the children's pets have disappeared. I've dispatched a squad to try to find its nest," Miss Cog said.

Ishe had to cover her mouth to hide the grin. Blinky had probably gone into the kitchen to beg for food. She could see it now. Blinky walking in, waving his middle legs in greeting, and then clicking in confusion when everyone screamed and ran away. Hopefully, the spider had nested somewhere no human could fit. Ishe risked a glance back at Yaki to share the moment, but her sister's nearly feral expression killed her own mirth. Yaki watched the food with the intensity of a starving tiger, gripping the railing of her hospital bed as if they were bars holding her back.

A servant brought Yaki a portion of food four times the size of everyone else's, and Yaz'noth watched with great interest as she made her food disappear, his head taking in the scene from multiple angles. Ishe's stomach tightened, fearing he'd spot the crystals as Yaki sat up, totally oblivious to the fact that her blanket had fallen away from her breasts. "Not much dignity now," Yaz'noth said with a lilt of amusement.

Yaki paused only to give Yaz'noth a rude gesture with her spoonless hand.

The dragon only chuckled.

Ishe ate her own food with only slightly less gusto. If Yaki needed that much food every three hours, then the logistics of their escape would be that much more complicated. And they had to do it before anyone changed Yaki's bedsheets.

Yaki finished her meal and slumped back onto her bed with the air of someone who had held her breath for a long time. "Please tell me the appetite will fade soon," Yaki said, wiping her mouth with the back of her hand.

"When you don't need the crystal, it will fade some. But I'm afraid the heart I made is less efficient than meat. In a month or so, after your sister returns from her errand, we will attempt to put your old heart back. A process that will be much easier if she manages to obtain a few more medical crystals." Yaz'noth glanced back at Ishe.

"I'll get them." Ishe nodded. *I'll get so many that once I rip out that thing you put inside her, a new heart will grow back so fast that she'll barely miss a beat.*

"See that you do. Now let's finish our task here." Yaz'noth returned to his position as Ishe resumed her task.

Chapter Thirty-Three

We don't call them spiders in our language. The term directly translates as "big fuzzy legs". Even the wild ones are friendly so long as you're too big to eat.

> — SEEK FIRE, CHIEF OF THE TURTLE
> CLAN OF THE LOW RIVERS TRIBE,
> LOREKEEPER

"SLEEP WHEN I'M DEAD," ISHE MUMBLED TO HERSELF. There were less than twelve hours left until the ship, *Scale*, was due to take her to the Golden Hills. Despite the exile of her family, she did not relish the idea of setting the residential district of her home on fire. If she fell asleep now, she wouldn't wake up until they were pushing her onto the airship or they found the crystals in Yaki's bed. Whichever came first. So, instead, she lay on her bunk, digging her nails deep into her palms and fighting to stay awake as she waited for the bunkroom to empty.

Finally, the shift change completed. The room fell into stillness accented with the breathing of slumbering people. After counting down the minutes, Ishe felt safe enough to ease out of bed. A young woman in a bunk by the door shifted as she walked past. Ishe stomped down to where the passage split off, one direction going toward Yaki's room and the other down farther to where the kitchens and food stores were. She took off her boots and proceeded down toward the kitchens. They were easy to find, at least. The smell of stew and mushrooms guided her bare feet. The Dragonsworn operated in three shifts, marked by hourglasses in different shades of sand posted in the bunkrooms. Now that the gray shift had begun, the halls were deserted. Ishe put her boots back on and began to tap out on the wall the code that had called Blinky before as she walked.

The cook, who was so far the only Dragonsworn Ishe had met who had any fat on his bones, smiled at her as she entered through the open doorway. Big meals happened at the end of each shift. Dragonsworn without a talon exchanged wooden tokens for their portions, and Ishe had a notion that food formed the foundation of what passed for an economy among them. Miners were paid double due to their hard labor. Blackcoats, mostly *Fox Fire*'s crew, got quarter rations unless they worked in the mines. Ishe's status as "blackcoat of interest to the Master" earned her freedom from the system, and the cook set a bowl of spiced mush on the bar he used to feed drop-ins. "On the Master's house," he said with a grin that was much larger than usual.

Ishe nodded and scanned the kitchen for the most portable foodstuff available. Stacked in the corner were pallets of rice bearing the Steward emblem. Rice harvested from the paddies of the Golden Hills. Two assistants were busying themselves making rice balls. A mountain goat turned on a huge spit. The meat seemed to be ever-present in the diet of the Dragonsworn. Either they truly had a huge herd or they were depleting them at a very quick rate.

The chef reached over an assistant to stick his finger in a bowl of something and taste it. "We've got the spices for now; don't use too little," he said, clapping the younger man on the back before turning to Ishe. "You'll miss this food when you get out to the Golden Hills or as we call them the Stolen Hills. They might have more greens, but I know thirty-seven ways to cook a ram."

"I heard you had a little excitement earlier." Ishe kept tapping with her toe as the man swaggered over.

"Yeah, cave spiders. Would you believe it? Big as an oven! We fought it off and sent it screaming for its mother." He smiled with pride and set his elbows on the bar in front of her. "You should have seen the fangs on it." He held out his finger and his thumb stretched apart and then decided he actually needed two hands. "Big as a butcher's knife!"

The assistant behind him visibly rolled his eyes.

"Do you get spiders down here that often?" Ishe worried that if she tapped any louder, people would start to notice, and began to reach for the knife inside her coat.

"Only in my great-grandma's stories," he said.

"Did they get bigger every time she told the story, too?" Ishe asked as her hand closed around the knife. *Could I cold-cock him instead?* she wondered as the inside of her palms grew damp. There'd been more than a few boarding actions resisted during the last two years, and Ishe's weapons had needed to be cleaned of blood several times. She told herself this would be no different. They were all keeping her and Yaki against their will. Mother had disapproved of mercy.

"Nah. Any bigger and they can't fit through the tunnels." He grinned. "Don't you worry, though!" He reached below the bar and came up with a heavy two-handed crossbow, the same type the guards in the mines had used. The weapon had been cocked, but no bolt rested on the bow. "That spider shows up and I'm going to learn how to make spider-on-a-stick."

A movement caught the corner of Ishe's eye as a dark shape pulled itself up onto the far end of the bar. Ishe fought every instinct to not to sigh with relief and instead focused on the cook's eyes. "Oh, really? What do you think a spider tastes like?"

"Like cave crawlers, I bet. Boil them with ram's butter," the chef said. Silent as a ghost, the eight-legged form of Blinky crept down the bar. "I bet those legs got plenty of meat in them. Serve those up to the three- and two-talons." Ishe bit her cheek to keep from smiling as Blinky got within leg's reach of the man.

The assistant turned around and froze, his eyes threatening to burst out of their sockets. His mouth flapping as he tried to find words. "B-b-b..."

"The rest of it can go into the stew. Everything goes in the stew." The chef's head began to turn.

"Boss!" the younger man wailed.

"Wha—" The chef finally saw Blinky no more than a foot away from his arm. Terror lit up his swollen face as he pushed himself away from the counter, only to topple backward, arms spinning like a slow-motion propeller. He let out a bloodcurdling scream as Blinky feinted jumping on the man, matching the yell with a high-pitched *scree* of his own. Ishe peered over the counter to see that the man's legs had been webbed together.

"Go get them, Blinky!" Ishe urged in a deep whisper.

Blinky scuttled toward the cook's assistant, flapping his second pair of legs like wings, and chittered madly. The man turned tail and bolted out the passageway.

Ishe grabbed a large chopping blade from the counter. "Go on!" she shouted at the two women who had been prepping the rice balls. "Go get help. I'll see if I can stab it."

They needed no more encouragement and ran for the opposite entryway. No sooner had they left than Ishe grabbed an empty rice sack and began stuffing it with as much food as she could grab. Adrenaline sang in her veins. It was now or never.

As she filled the sack, Blinky amused himself with the poor chef by batting at the man like a cat with a mouse. Once the sack bulged, she tossed the spider a cut of raw goat. Blinky snatched it up and was on her heels as she ran from the room.

"Giant spider!" she screamed as she ran, Blinky gleefully clicking behind her. A pair of guards came rushing up toward her, both sporting batons. Ishe clotheslined the first and slammed the other into the rock wall of the passage.

Neither managed to get back up as the tunnel curved away.

Chapter Thirty-Four

❧

Sometimes, the cleverest trick is a punch to the nose.

— ADMIRAL MADRIA, DURING HER
FIRST AND ONLY LECTURE AT THE
GOLDEN HILLS NAVAL ACADEMY

YAKI WOKE TO HYSTERICAL SCREAMS ECHOING INTO HER room. "About time," she said to herself, and climbed out of bed. No sooner had her feet touched the cold stone did Madam Ye's tiny form appear in the doorway, flanked by a much larger man who actually filled it. Yaki forced herself to unclench her fists at the sight of the guard. While she'd happily toss the mean old nurse aside, the guard would be much more difficult.

"What are you doing out of bed?" Madam Ye snapped.

"What's all the screaming about?" Yaki countered.

"Nothing for you to worry about. It's being handled." Ye brandished her cane at Yaki. "Back to bed, young lady."

Yaki huffed and began to ease herself back onto the bed as she tried to decide whether to comply or to charge the old woman with her loaded pillowcase.

The guard's head snapped to the left just in time to receive a fist to his nose. The strike came with a distinct "Ha!" that only Ishe made when she hit people. The guard reeled back out of the doorway as Ishe stepped into it. Her boot lashed out low, and the man toppled back into view only for Ishe to catch him by the hair. His forehead made a loud, hollow *crack* as Ishe drove it into the corner of the entryway.

Madam Ye turned just in time to watch the guard fall bonelessly from Ishe's grip. Seeing no other option, Yaki snatched up her pillow in preparation to smack the old woman senseless.

Too slow. "Nasty, no-good girl!" Madam Ye, wielding her cane like a two-handed sword, tried to crack Ishe's skull like an egg as she walked in the door. Ishe brushed the stick aside with a sweep of her arm, locking it against her torso. Her hand enveloped Madam Ye's wrist and jerked the small woman up onto her toes. Yaki winced as Ishe drove a fist into the elderly woman's midsection. "Ooooof." Ye exhaled and crumpled to the floor, making tiny gasping noises.

"You scream before we leave and I will shatter your skull," Ishe told the woman as she pulled the insensate guard inside the room. "Get the crystals out of that bed, Yaki; we gotta go." Kneeling, she started to undo the buttons of the man's coat.

Yaki stepped behind the bed and unscrewed the clamps that held the medical crystal in place. The crystal dimmed as she lifted it free of its setting. Pain flared in her chest and forced a hiss from her lungs.

"What now?" Ishe asked as she peeled the boneless guard out of his jacket.

"One moment." Yaki examined the metal headboard; it had several panels held closed with small pivoting latches. She popped them open one by one.

"We don't have a moment." Ishe placed the brown coat over her sister's shoulders as the last panel was pried open. A soft blue glow shone out from the oblong crystal contained within. Aside from the glow, the crystal was transparent. Ishe raised her eyebrows. "A power crystal?"

"They're boosting the medical crystal with it. That's why it's so cracked. It's not good for it." Yaki plucked the stone from the socket and held it to the medical crystal. The pain in her chest vanished. She shoved them into one of the pockets of the purloined jacket. The other one bulged with something else, probably lunch. The red of the medical crystal peeked out the top.

"Well, that fixes one problem," Ishe said. "We can see by that."

"Eeeeeeee." A wheeze of a scream came from the old woman as an eight-legged form skittered under the top of the entryway.

"Blinky!" Yaki's heart click-clanged as the spider scuttled across the ceiling. He dropped on top of her just as she got her arms through the sleeves of the coat. She briefly staggered under the weight of the many-limbed embrace as he hung on to her front. She gave him a brief scratch. "Who's a good spider? Blinky is! Yes, you are!"

The monstrosity that had so terrified the Dragonsworn churned happily.

"That's a pet?" Madam Ye wheezed.

"And that's our cue to leave." Yaki managed to stagger over to the bed, grabbed the pillow loaded with crystals, and slung it over her shoulder.

Ishe pitched her voice low. "Okay, Blinky! Find Sparrow."

The spider bobbed and jumped down to the ground.

Chittering, he scuttled toward the door. Ishe scooped up the guard's spear and a large sack as the sisters followed.

Chapter Thirty-Five

❦

I hunt dragons. I am not afraid of spiders. Except the ones the Northern tribes ride. The sound they make when they eat..."

— SHINTO YASAMOTO, AUTHOR OF
DRAGON HUNTING WITHOUT DYING

Ishe decided she never ever wanted to meet Blinky's wild cousins or an unfriendly ship spider. He scurried on the ceiling, and whenever they saw anyone, he'd charge with a feral *SCREEEE*, flapping legs, and flashing fangs. To a one, the Dragonsworn would shriek and run away, either the way they came or diving into side passages. Ishe would heft her spear and make like Yaki and her were chasing after Blinky, warning of larger ones in the tunnels above. Soon, the Dragonsworn stopped appearing and Blinky skittered into an unlit tunnel. The spider stopped, and Ishe could hear Blinky's breath as a chorus of whistles.

A soft blue glow blossomed in the tunnel as Yaki held the power crystal in her hand up to her heart. "It's not going to jump out, is it? Your heart, I mean," Ishe said.

"No." Yaki shook her head. "It's loud, though. You can't hear it?"

"You're breathing louder than it's beating," Ishe said, checking up and down the tunnel. "So, here's the plan. Sparrow and Hawk know where there are ventilation shafts. We get—"

"And you blow a hole in the side of the mountain. I figured that part out," Yaki said, shaking the bag.

"You didn't see the scenery coming in; these mountains are covered with a dense forest. We'll be in the trees as soon as we're out." Ishe pushed off the wall. "Come on. We need to keep moving." She got three steps before she realized Yaki hadn't budged.

Ishe turned. "You said you'd rather die than go through that…surgery again. Don't tell me you're having second thoughts?"

"I could slow them down. I'm dead already, Ishe. I could —" Yaki began.

Ishe took two steps, snatched her sister's pretty little hand, pulled her off the wall, and started marching down the tunnel. There was no time for those thoughts.

"Ahh!" Yaki stumbled to follow.

"You can moan about how you're going to die soon after you get a diagnosis from an actual doctor from Lyndon. Not a dragon who cuts up his servants because he's bored!" Ishe hissed, releasing Yaki's wrist and shoving her forward into the gloom.

Blinky clicked and scuttled ahead. The crystals on his abdomen glowed a dull red, just enough to track him in the dark.

"But—" Yaki protested while she walked.

"We get out and we stick together," Ishe said.

"And then what?" Yaki said, picking her way along in her bare feet.

"We'll figure it out. Worse comes to worst, we become the most successful muggers Golden Hills has ever seen. You blind merchants with your smile and I'll take their wallets." Ishe grinned.

Yaki huffed. "Fine. Tell me what we're walking into down here."

Ishe told her all about the visit to Hawk, Sparrow, and the rest of the crew. Particularly the part about the ten men with crossbows standing guard.

Blinky led them deeper into the mountain through passageways that had been long abandoned. Empty sockets in the ceiling revealed that once upon a time, there might have been a lot more Dragonsworn. The architecture was quite different from the warrens above. Instead of a passage with rooms branching off from the side, tunnels through the rock linked roughly rectangular chambers, their floors covered with loose rubble. Occasionally, the dim light of the power crystal would shine on some hint of human habitation, a broken ax shaft, a cast-off boot, but the surroundings remained still and dead as they hurried through. Slowly, the chambers grew larger; stone supports appeared and then thickened as they reached a chamber that had the clammy chill of a graveyard.

The light of the power crystal began to flicker softly in response to Yaki's trembling hand. Ishe gripped Yaki's shoulder as footsteps began to echo behind them. Hollow clacks of bone against rock. Neither said a word. The dead would either take issue with their trespass or not. They had nothing to appease them with.

Another few chambers and the sound of the pursuit died away. Ishe muttered a prayer of thanks. The rooms were now recognizable as quarries, and Ishe had an inkling of where they were. They'd been walking through the evolution of the Dragonsworn mining and now were wending their way around the central shaft, a series of back tunnels that linked the quarries to each other. Although they hurried on, Ishe couldn't be sure if the ringing of a distant alarm bell was in her imagination or real. She wondered if they should run to the central shaft and slide down the chains.

Still, they were making good time. Until Blinky led them to a collapsed passage filled entirely with rubble. The spider didn't pause. He crawled over the loose stone and slipped his front legs between two that looked too close together. But with a little wriggle, he disappeared into the pile.

"*Tic-tic*," Blinky clicked after Ishe and Yaki failed to follow him.

"Tell me there's another way." Yaki stepped up onto the pile of rubble to peer into the hole. Her head might fit, but that would be about it.

"We'll have to take the main route." Ishe nodded and gestured to her sister before turning to follow the wall. After a few twists and turns, they reached the central shaft. Stepping out onto the scaffold, Ishe saw why Yaz'noth had been so keen to keep Earth crystals out of the hands of his miners. Beneath her feet, the structure vibrated with the force of boots hammering the steps above. They might not know where they were, but they had a good idea where Ishe and Yaki would be heading.

Shaking her arm, Ishe dropped a few of the remaining Earth crystals out of her sleeve and onto her palm. "Here, take the spear and give me the power crystal."

Yaki made the trade with a worried expression. "What are you doing?"

"Slowing them down. Start . I'll catch up." Ishe climbed up a dozen steps. The scaffold was supported every four steps with an I beam of thin metal bolted into the rock. Ishe leaned out over one with Earth crystals in one hand and the power crystal in the other.

"Have you snapped your masts?" Yaki hissed.

"Nope. Just snapping this scaffold." Ishe tapped the power crystal to the Earth crystals before dropping them. They fell from her hand, flaring into a brilliant jade light.

Yaki clutched at the medical crystal in her pocket and leaped down the next flight of stairs.

"You're overreacting!" Ishe called out. Two of the crystals bounced free of the support, but one rolled down its length like a lucky gambler's die, stopping once it nestled in the V formed between the metal and the rock wall. One by one, the crystals popped like a cluster of New Year's firecrackers. The metal squealed as if in pain, bucking beneath Ishe's feet before sagging. The lucky crystal had blown clean through the support. "We stop them here and they'll have to either dig out that passage or go all the way back up to shimmy down the chain," Ishe called to her sister. "Give me more crystals."

Stepping gingerly, Yaki trod back up the steps. "We better not go down with it, Rhino."

"Trust me." Ishe snatched the pillowcase containing the crystals and dug several out. Her aim was better the second time, and she managed to take out two supports with the same number of crystals. The entire flight of stairs hung free of the supports, only the railings remaining anchored. It looked more like a rope bridge than a metal scaffolding. Ishe pumped a fist at her handiwork. "Ha! Now, that will slow them down."

"It's slowing us down," Yaki said. She grabbed Ishe's hand, and together they began to descend the staircase. "What if they heard that?"

Ishe said nothing as the din of the picks and drills drifted up from below. They waited until they were about two stories above the dock of the current quarry and ducked into a side passage. Ishe had been expecting this to be another spent quarry, but as she stepped through the doorway, the distinct scent of unwashed humanity slapped her in the face. She stopped so suddenly, Yaki walked right into her back. The dim light of the power crystal revealed the silhouettes of bunks crammed against the walls of the chamber.

"Wazzit light for? It can't be our shift yet," someone muttered.

Ishe's mind froze for a brief moment, and only when Yaki tugged her back toward the stairway did she dig in her heels. She shook her sister off and swallowed back the bitter taste of panic. Retreat would give them away. Instead, she straightened herself and asked in her most commanding voice, "Where is Hawk? Is she on shift?"

"What? The big one, right?" someone else answered sleepily.

"The Master wants to see her. *Now,*" Ishe said, striding forward, not waiting for an actual reply as she crossed the room to the opposite entrance.

"Good luck telling her to do anything." Someone sniggered, but Ishe and Yaki was already on the other side of the room and crossing into a hallway heading toward the main quarry. Behind them, someone laughed.

Passing under the blanket that hung over the doorway of the Dragonsworn bunkhouse, they entered a short hallway. Actual wooden doors guarded the rooms to the left and right. A thin sheet rippled at the far end of the hall, and Ishe could see the outline of a figure standing in front. Elbowing her sister, she whispered, "Be my escort."

Yaki nodded silently, handed Ishe the pillowcase full of crystals, and plucked the spear from her hand.

Chapter Thirty-Six

The Steward said the Golden Hills would not bow to any reptile, metal or not. He ordered twenty tons of iron cast into ingots as bait.

— SHINTO YASAMOTO, AUTHOR OF
DRAGON HUNTING WITHOUT DYING

YAKI HEFTED THE SPEAR IN HER HAND AND FELT ITS weight. It was surprisingly light for something made entirely out of metal. She did her level best to ignore both the growing pain in her chest and the harsh *ka-chink, ka-chink* of her heart.

Showtime, she told herself as she rolled her shoulders and experienced the familiar dread that filled her whenever Mother had her perform. Whether it was being distractedly pretty for a customs agent or singing for a gaggle of nobles, the dread had been a constant companion.

"Coming through." She pitched her voice low, trying to

imitate Ishe's commanding baritone as she shoved the curtain aside. The man swiftly stepped aside with barely a glance in her direction before doing a double take, his eyes narrowing at the crown of Yaki's head.

Oh, shit, my hair! Yaki's grip tightened on the spear, but before she could even decide what to do with it, Ishe had her arm around the guard's neck. With the swiftness of a snake, she pulled him back behind the curtain.

A few muffled thumps were the only evidence of struggle afterward.

Yaki turned away and took in her surroundings. This quarry had been converted into a barracks for the miners. Like all the others above, every fifty feet or so, a five-foot-wide pillar stretched between the floor and ceiling in a grid-like pattern. Glow crystals sparsely dotted the space. In the center of the room, a six-by-two-yard area of the quarry was cordoned off with iron bars a hand's width apart. Both in and outside the pen were clusters of metal bunks. It appeared that all the miners, blackcoats and browncoats, slept in this room. The majority of the at-liberty bunks appeared empty, however. Word of their escape had not yet reached the mines. More evidence that the Dragonsworn were unaccustomed to keeping prisoners.

Yaki leaned the spear against the wall and tried to slick back the many strands of hair that had escaped her long braid. Ishe's familiar presence came up behind her.

"Leave it; don't get close," Ishe whispered.

"And if they do?" Yaki asked.

"We hit them. Go on," Ishe said with coldness that sounded a lot like Mother discussing strategy.

Squaring her shoulders, Yaki strode out toward the pen, having no idea what to do next. A guard sat a pillar away from it, fiddling with his crossbow. He raised his head to peer at her and Yaki turned aside, putting pillars between her and the guard at the entryway to the barracks.

"Find Hawk," Ishe urged.

Yaki bit back a snappish reply. Hawk wasn't in the pen. She'd never fit in one of those bunks. A ragged cough echoed off the stone, identifying the presence of Sparrow in the room. She wished Blinky had followed them out to the central shaft. Without the spider as a backup plan, she felt exposed, and her scalp now prickled. Two guards sat in chairs by the gate to the pen. Between them, the large form of a juvenile dragon, wider than the door, lay curled. Copper scales shifted in the dim light as it snoozed. That would not be an entrance.

Yaki tore her eyes away and focused on a more intense glow in the back corner of the quarry, where the passage to the next chamber lay. No guards stood at the passage, which glowed brightly in Yaki's vision from the number of glow crystals that dotted its walls. They passed through the doorway into another quarry, this one set up as an equipment warehouse and guarded by two men who sat behind desks. Racks of overalls, picks, shovels, and drills lined the walls. Empty ore carts filled the space between the pillars. One looked up at Yaki as she strode in, eyes squinting in either suspicion or nearsightedness, yet he did not call out or stop them.

The next chamber, however, stopped Yaki dead in her tracks. A dozen dragons rested among the pillars. The largest was the size of a horse. The smallest would have its shoulder reach her waist. They ran in color from the dark hues of cold iron to polished silver, to the dull gleam of copper. Only the smaller ones had any wings at all, but they looked stumpy and vestigial. Around their necks were looped thin chains that had been padlocked to a wall or pillar.

"Stop staring and keep moving," Ishe said.

"We have to go back for Sparrow," Yaki whispered. "Not even Hawk will be able to get through this many dragons."

"They'll have a plan of their own. Trust me." Ishe nudged her forward. Yaki shot her sister a glare but resumed moving. Her speed increased as several dragon heads snaked toward them with interest.

"This is the last time I let you plan our escape route," Yaki whispered.

Ishe chuckled. "As if I had any time to plan anything."

One more chamber, this one thick with the smell of food. Tables and chairs had been set up between the pillars, and a long buffet could be seen near the entrance. The clatter of industrious noise came from the doorways nearer to the central shaft. Yaki's stomach churned as she walked into a cloud of pulverized rock that drifted up the passage.

The din of the mining grew into a cacophony as they reached the active quarry. Dozens of men and women worked on a wall of stone with pickaxes, while others shoveled what they pulled loose into metal carts hauled by horse-sized dragons. The room had been cut out lengthwise, and compared to the other chambers, it was about half-size. Teams of brown-coated Dragonsworn with a peppering of blackcoats worked along the wall in hundred-foot intervals. A shrill buzz screamed through the space, and Yaki found Hawk in the central section. She wielded one of the massive drills by herself. A thick cable protruded from the back of the drill that connected to a glass canister containing a ship-sized power crystal about a third the size of Julia. The blue glow had a purplish tint to it, marking it as one unhappy crystal. The poor thing.

None of the guards noticed either Yaki or Ishe, focused instead on their individual charges; each work crew had one. Except for Hawk's—her team had three guards, all armed with loaded crossbows. What now?

Swallowing down her panic, Yaki marched over sharp rocks toward Hawk. The Amazonian woman stopped drilling and heaved the bit back from the stone wall. Several of the blackcoats did a double take as Yaki and Ishe walked by, their eyes staring at a space a couple of paces behind the sisters. Yaki glanced behind and saw a trail of huge paw prints in the dust behind her, their path ending right next to her, the exact same size as the mark on her shoulder. They had to abort, right now. Whirling back around, she reached to grab Ishe's coat and haul her away. Ishe did not budge. Her eyes had found Hawk's.

The huge woman smirked. That was all the warning her guards got before her drill smashed into two of them. The third had his crossbow swatted aside before her foot drove him into the wall with the snapping of bones.

A stunned silence rippled out from around Hawk as the miners took in the blood-soaked coats of the men she had killed.

Hawk snatched up a shovel, and grin glowed with the malice of a wild bird contained. With a feral keening, she threw the shovel like a spear at a Dragonsworn who had dared to raise his bow. The shovel split the crossbow in twain, biting deep into the man's chest. "Kill all who stand!" she boomed.

The mine erupted into chaos. The sole dragon who had been hauling rock screamed like a rabbit and bolted toward the door, dragging his handlers with him. Some Dragonsworn took the hint and dived to the floor, but the majority of the miners, black and brown, turned on each other with savage ferocity as if they had been waiting for this moment. Picks and shovels punched through skulls and split kneecaps. Ishe ripped the spear out of Yaki's frozen hands and drove it through the eye of a Dragonsworn who had gotten too close. The browncoats fell. Madria's crew struck without mercy or hesitation. The first mate had spoken and she would be obeyed.

In the span of seconds, not a single Dragonsworn stood. They lay on the floor either quivering with fear or still in a puddle of blood.

Yaki's head reeled from the dizzying speed of the violence. Now over, it echoed through her head as if her skull was as hollow as the mountain. Ishe caught her as she stumbled.

"Were you hit?" Ishe asked.

"No. Ishe, did they need to do…do it that way?" she said in a low whisper. Already knowing the answer. Dreading it.

"That's the way Mother trained them…and me," Ishe said. "Now you better stand up and smile."

"You didn't kill the guard and the woman," Yaki said, sucking in her breath.

"And Hawk didn't kill those who surrendered." Ishe pushed Yaki off her with a hip.

Yaki found herself in Hawk's shadow. The giant woman knelt, her hand gently cupping Yaki's chin and forcing her to look up into Hawk's eyes. Shadowed, they looked like deep pits.

"Did that dragon take your name? Do I need to go get it back?" Hawk asked.

Yaki remembered the feeling of being shattered between teeth and the embrace of fur around her. "No." She shivered as the mark on her back tingled. "The Flower is dead." Her voice sounded strange as heat and light flared behind her. Yaki jerked her head from Hawk's grip to see flames lick up her shoulder.

"Rotten iron!" Hawk slapped out the flame with a single back clap that Yaki felt all the way to her toes. The powerful hands spun her as if she were nothing more than a doll. A moment passed, and Yaki felt Hawk's eyes boring into the mark. "I see. We will talk about this later. Never cover this mark up unless you wear it on your clothing as well. That is not a spirit you want to anger." The hands released her, and Yaki found herself stumbling without their support. "The crew will show you to the ventilation shaft. I need to get my husband. Do not wait."

Hawk moved. The towering woman from Low Rivers grabbed a pickax in each hand and ran, not for the tunnel Ishe and Yaki had come down but for the central shaft. Distantly, a cold voice in Yaki's head calculated that Hawk had chosen to go through all the guards in the bunkhouse rather than the dozen dragons. Yaki pitied those guards.

Chapter Thirty-Seven

🌿

Of all the Dragons in the Seven Saved Lands, only the White Queen was larger than Yaz'noth. Born sometime in the later half of the Great Wyrm's Empire, Yaz'noth reached adulthood in time to witness its decline.

> — HON NISHAMURA, CHIEF
> HISTORIAN OF THE STEWARD'S
> ARCHIVES

ISHE GROWLED AS HER USELESS SISTER STARED OFF AFTER Hawk. No wonder Mother stuffed her into the engine room at the first sign of trouble. Far too delicate for the bloody business that was privateering. This was what they were. It was better for her to finally see the truth. Even in the stories, the bad guys died in droves. Grabbing Yaki's arm, she pulled her toward a clustering of crewmates who were muttering about seeing a big cat. "Where's the ventilation shaft?"

One of them, a man nicknamed Diggy for a nose-picking

habit he had since kicked, gestured back toward the corner passage. "Over here." He led them back to the far corner of the quarry, a few feet from the passage that led up to the chamber where all the dragons slumbered. There, hidden by an outcropping of rock and so low that you practically had to be on your knees to see it, was a tunnel. Ishe waved her hand in front of it and felt a cool breeze blowing in. Squinting, she could see a faint light, far away.

"Goes in about a hundred feet," Diggy volunteered, "then goes straight up. Dunno how far, but you can see sunlight through that hole."

Not enough. The thought pierced through Ishe's mind and exploded into a cloud of dread. Two shells' worth of Earth crystals would blow a huge hole in a rock wall, but the chunk of rock melted away by the blast would be measured in tens of feet, not the hundreds it might take to get through the side of the mountain.

How much time did they have before Yaz'noth crawled down that central shaft, fit his lips to that entryway, and filled the entire quarry with flame? Ishe searched for a solution. Her eyes first fell on the barrels of black powder. No, that would just bring the entire quarry down on their heads. Then she saw the crystal that they'd been using to power the drills. Housed in a huge glass casing, it emitted a light that cast an angry glare over the part of the quarry where it resided. In its blue light she could see the explosion that had torn *Fox Fire* apart. With it, she remembered Koshue explaining the workings of the elemental lance, the weapon she never had the chance to use. They were simple things. A massive amount of power was channeled through an elemental crystal, which projected that energy into a beam. If you wanted to reuse your elemental crystal, it had to be of very high quality. But if you only needed one shot…then a lens of ammo crystals might serve.

Ishe grabbed her sister by the shoulders. Yaki looked pale, like someone who'd spent the night communing with ancestors in the catacombs. "They're not going to make it, Ishe," she mumbled. "The Death Panther's here."

"Would that have stopped Mom?" Ishe growled. "What did she say about signs and portents?"

Yaki grimaced. "They're warnings, not fate. Even spirits can be wrong." Ishe saw a flash of Mother's steel in her sister's eyes as she recentered from her daze.

"Can a power crystal project a beam without an emitter?" Ishe asked.

"Not a good one, but yes, they can be convinced." Yaki's eyes flicked to the large crystal, then to the tunnel. Understanding flared in her eyes. "Power alone won't be enough to—"

Ishe snatched the bag of Earth crystals from Yaki hand and held it up.

"That...that might work," Yaki concluded.

Ishe turned and began to shout orders to the milling blackcoats, who were eager to do something, anything.

They quickly brought over an empty black powder barrel. Ishe added a few shovelfuls of pulverized rock to the bag of crystals to give it a little more volume, mixed them up, and jammed the bag into the mouth of the barrel. They pried off the bottom and slid it into the ventilation tunnel. It fit, barely. That would be their lens.

Meanwhile, another team working under Yaki repositioned the big power crystal. Pickaxes made short work of the glass housing, and the cave filled with the noise of a thousand screaming wasps.

YAKI KNELT, STRETCHING HER HANDS OUT TOWARD THE

large crystal. It stung her fingers with arcs of power and filled her head with its rage. The soothing thoughts Yaki sent to it were slapped back as insulting. It railed against the years of powering mere tools. Yaki felt herself flow and stretch through a massive liftwood hull. Her heart swelled with pride as she alone powered it, pushed it into the sky. The effort taxed her, made premature cracks in her surface, but she had done it. Done all by herself.

And now. Now all they wanted from her were these piddly little drills? How boring. How insulting. She had lifted a grand ship into the sky! Togi would show them. Togi would run those drills until they shattered from his great power!

Pulling her fingers back, Yaki broke the connection to the crystal. She ran her hand through her greasy hair and collected herself. She reminded herself that she was Yaki and not Togi. Julia had been nothing like this. *Fox Fire*'s crystal had wanted to be coddled and encouraged. It had been a child to nurture. This Togi before her was a beast that needed to be contained. In its anger, it had run roughshod over her very awareness.

"Did it burn you?" a sailor asked.

Yaki checked her hands and found blisters at the end of her fingers. Rotten iron; Mother would kill her if they scarred. Then she remembered where she was and that Madria had supposedly died. She cursed out loud.

"Are you all right?" the sailor asked again. Yaki glanced at her face, composed of dark weathered skin. The bright, alert eyes were scanning Yaki's face, and worry creased her brow.

Yaki did not know the name of this sailor and bit back an urge to ask if she had seen the Death Panther. Instead, she told the woman that she was fine, cracked her neck to gather her wits, and reached back out to the crystal.

How would you like to change the face of a mountain, Togi?

she thought at it, sending images of a mountain falling in on itself.

Togi's angry hum shifted in tone to that of a droning question. It stopped lashing power at her fingers. A note of interest sounded. Yaki smiled. She directed the black-coated crewmembers around her to pick up Togi, but the crystal objected, repelling their reaching hands with tiny bolts of power.

"Make a sling with your coats!" she said. Two coats were laid down, and Yaki personally rolled the crystal onto them. Four sailors took the sleeves and hauled the crystal over to the mouth of the ventilation tunnel.

"How long will it take to do this?" Ishe asked as Yaki knelt beside the crystal.

"I don't know!" Yaki snapped. "I've never asked a crystal to blow itself up before." She reached out to Togi and closed her eyes. "Just give me a moment or two."

"I'm not sure how many moments we have left," Ishe answered.

Chapter Thirty-Eight

✿◉✿

Yaz'noth's teeth are steel; I remember seeing my own panicked reflection in his grin as he dove on my ship. The flames that followed cooked my eyeballs. Now that image of myself in him is frozen in my mind.

— SHINTO YASAMOTO, AUTHOR OF
DRAGON HUNTING WITHOUT DYING

THERE WERE NARROWED REPTILIAN EYES PEEKING DOWN at them from the top of the passage. A broad copper muzzle bared a set of serrated teeth as its nostrils flared.

Ishe threw her spear; it flew through the air and bounced off the dragon's head, which pulled back out of view with a yip. "Yaki, those dragons are getting curious." Ishe picked up a large stone and several blackcoats mirrored her.

"Trying..." Yaki's voice was strained.

"Bad Blackcoats. No good." The dragon that Miss Cog had addressed as Smooge popped his head around the corner and hissed. Several rocks flew from the hands of sailors. "Fry them, Nidge! You burn best. Burn them to bones!"

The copper dragon appeared and belched forth a wave of white flame. It filled the passage entirely and the intense heat drove Ishe back, nearly tripping over Yaki's foot.

"Yaki, things are starting to heat up here!" Ishe said. A crewmember came up beside her with a loaded crossbow.

"Please don't try to pun." Yaki groaned as a spider web of fractures spread over the surface of the crystal. "Come on, Togi, you can do it." Small stones around it were drifting into the air.

"Yes!" Smooge urged. "Closer!"

Nidge hissed like an angry snake as he inched into full view. The crossbow fired with a loud *thwhip!* The bolt shot into Nidge's shoulder and stuck. With a screech, the dragon backed out of sight. "They have flying pokes! Am I bad?!" a raspy voice asked.

"No, Nidge good! Blackcoats bad. Smell that blood! They stole the very bad pokers. Burn them!" Smooge urged.

"I don't like pokers!" Nidge's voice answered.

Ishe gestured as the crew rushed to gather up the crossbows.

"Smooge burn them, then! Follow!" The dragon's head poked around the corner and breathed forth a flame. It didn't come anywhere close to Ishe and Yaki, but it obscured the passage with orange light. When the flames collapsed, they could see that Smooge had advanced into the tunnel.

"Fire!" Ishe shouted.

Thwhip! Three crossbow bolts flew. Two plinked off his silver scales, but one thudded deep in his leg. Smooge bared his teeth. "Poke Smooge all you want! Smooge will burn you anyway! You bad!" He blasted out another cone of fire. Two more dragons crept up behind him: Nidge and another with iron scales like Yaz'noth.

"Here it goes!" Yaki shouted. "Everyone get clear!"

Ishe glanced behind her as the crystal's whine blotted out everything else. The crystal shone: first blue, then flashing to green as the rock around it began to glow with intense orange heat. Yaki beat it for a solid wall, and this time, Ishe nearly tripped over her own toes sprinting after her sister.

Whoosh! Ishe had made it halfway behind the wall when a great force slammed into the exposed half of her body and sent her spinning into a cart behind Yaki. The cart rocked onto two wheels and then fell back down, roughly dumping Ishe to the ground. Green light filled her vision, which for a moment began to fade at the edges.

"Run for it!" Yaki's hand was in hers, pulling her up. Ishe blinked as a too-bright circle searing into her retinas— daylight. Shaking her head, she looked again. The daylight shone at the end of a perfectly round tunnel. Green wisps of energy still danced over the surface of the rock walls.

"Heeeeehaaaaaaas!" Came a cry as a boxy shape careened down from the passage. A mining cart filled with screaming people and a figure that could only be Hawk standing on the back. As the cart hit the bottom of the slope, a metal wheel snapped away. The cart tipped over lengthwise, spilling its cargo of people and one very large spider. Hawk, who had merely stepped off the back, scooped Sparrow up with the grace of an eagle snatching a fish. Husband secured, she ran down the tunnel. "Follow me!" Her voice echoed in her wake. Blinky skittered after his master with frantic clicking.

With a whoop and cheer, all the blackcoats followed. Ishe found herself in a crowd as they booked it for freedom. Up ahead, Hawk and Sparrow passed into the light. The sunlight revealing their coats to be a chalky gray.

Ishe entered the tunnel in the middle of the pack, and only her height allowed her to keep an eye on Hawk's back. Out of the tunnel, Hawk's body dipped from view. Just as her head plunged under the tunnel's horizon, the sunlight shining on Hawk's black hair disappeared and the world outside dimmed for a moment.

The first bunch of sailors exited the tunnel into a torrent of blue flame pouring on them from above. Ishe skidded to a stop, plowing into the person in front of her. Screams erupted both from the crew inside and outside the tunnel.

Those blackcoats near the entrance stopped and stared at their companions who writhed in flames. Ishe pushed against them, "Keep going!" she urged them. "Before he can circle around!"

Yet the men and women in front of her remained a wall of flesh, frozen in place by fear. More people pressed up against her back. Snarling with frustration, Ishe rocked herself backward and hurled herself headfirst into the clog of people. The impact knocked two people flat onto their faces as she burst into the glorious sunlight and rolled down the hill. The world spun in a dance of rough earth and sky until her midsection found a very solid tree trunk.

"Ishe!" Yaki's voice screamed.

Rolling away from the trunk that had so suddenly stopped her tumble, Ishe's vision filled with the spindly branches of evergreens. Above, the shape of Yaz'noth plunging from the sky was unmistakable.

"Ishe!" the cry came again.

Rolling up to her hands and knees, Ishe saw her sister stuck in the press of people at the very edge of the tunnel. Several crewmates were still trying to get into the "safety" of the mountain and were blocking everyone else from escaping. Ishe forced herself to her feet and bellowed, but the men and woman panicked by the flaming bodies of their comrades remained deaf.

Finally, the head of the largest man gumming up the works rocked back. Someone had clocked him squarely in the nose. Black-coated men and woman stumbled out of the hole and down the mountainside as Yaz'noth's shadow grew rapidly. Yaki staggered out right before the dragon hit the stone face above the tunnel. He twisted in midair so all four feet hit at once. The impact rained pulverized stone on the fleeing crew of *Fox Fire*. Turning swiftly, Yaz'noth slammed one massive paw down on the tunnel entrance like a cat blocking a mouse hole, his metallic claws barely missing Yaki, now free of the mob. Several of the crew were not so lucky.

Yet unlike the others, Yaki did not break into a run. Instead, she took a few halting steps forward before falling to her knees. Hands clutched at her chest, then pocket, as she pulled out the medical crystal. Dead and dull like the Fire crystals Ishe had scattered on the floor. She smashed it into her chest.

Yaz'noth settled down behind her, deliberately stopping up the tunnel with his bulk. With a vicious grin, he opened his mouth and a terrible blue light shone from the back of his throat. The same beam he had used to destroy *Fox Fire* lanced out and, with a sweep of his head, cut through five fleeing people. They fell to the ground in ten charred pieces.

The golden eyes met Ishe's. The light grew bright and Ishe steeled herself for death. The beam shot out, but several feet to her left. Someone deeper in the forest screamed.

He smiled at her before turning toward another of her fleeing crewmates. This time, the beam was aimed directly in front of one of the men, Xi, who had been part of her cannon crew. He had no time to stop. His own momentum sliced him in twain.

Two more victims fell before Ishe found her voice. "Stop! Please stop!"

The dragon closed his mouth, but the blue death light leaked between his teeth. "Oh, now you wish to talk." He laughed. "And why should I talk to one who breaks their deals? And murders their allies?"

"We're not allies! You killed my mother. I will never obey you!" Ishe spat, her vision blurring with tears.

"Perhaps you should rethink that." The beam lashed out down the mountain and harvested another last scream. "How many are you willing to let die for your stubbornness, Little Rhino?"

"Don't you call me that! Don't you ever call me that." Ishe searched the ground for a weapon, for anything at all. She snatched up a jagged rock and threw it with all her might. "Ha!"

The rock hit Yaz'noth in the chest, bounced off his metallic hide, and dropped squarely onto Yaki's head.

"Ah!" Yaki cried, and crumpled to the ground. One hand flew up to grasp at the latest wound; the other still pried at her chest.

The dragon threw his head back and made the earth shake with the boom of his laughter. "HA! HA! HA! HA! HA!"

"Yaki!" Ishe took several steps toward her sister before Yaz'noth's head swung back down and blasted a line of flame in front of her. The blistering heat drove her back to the trees. "I'm sorry," she said under her breath.

"You stay put," said the dragon, still chuckling to himself. "I had been preparing an entire lecture since I saw you slipping those crystals down your sleeve. However, that rock illustrated the concept of our relationship very well."

"You knew?" Ishe covered her mouth and her body began to tremble. He'd known all along? But why hadn't he stopped her? Why the waste? The dragon merely smiled back as he sighted on something unseen and breathed forth another beam of blue death that scythed through the wood. A distant yell of pain. There was nothing she could do. No weapons to make him stop. No words to make him fear her.

He killed another. "I can do this all day. I know where they all are. There are twenty-one people still trapped in the mountain. Nine more are cowering in the woods, and the big one"—he squinted—"and little Sparrow are still running. They're out of range, but that's very fixable." He stretched out his wings.

"What do you want from me?" Ishe shouted up at the dragon.

"For you and your sister to understand consequences. Do you understand them now? Do you need further demonstrations?" Blue fire leaked from his lips and fell dangerously close to Yaki.

Biting her lip and digging her fingers into her palms, she grasped for something, anything that might give her some options. Mother would pull out some hidden trick or alliance. Reveal that the dragon had exposed himself to his enemies. But there was nothing. She had been operating at the very limit of what she could do and still had failed. Ishe imagined her mother's gasp of horror as she knelt before the dragon. "You win, Yaz'noth." Her breath shuddered. "I'll get your quicksilver." Her eyes fell to Yaki, for whom breathing had become a struggle.

The dragon shook his head. "No. You've had your chance. Partially my fault. I set up the wrong incentives. But I've squared them now." He lowered his head to the gasping Yaki. A massive claw curled around her neck and forced her chin upward. "How about we try this one on for size? Are you listening, Yaki?"

Yaki swallowed and nodded minutely.

"You will go, in your sister's place, to the Golden Hills and retrieve my quicksilver. Ishe will stay as my personal guest. For every month that goes by without your return, I will replace a piece of her, the same way I replaced your heart. Except I will make it truly hurt. I'll start small, a finger or a tongue, and I'll work my way up to the internal organs," Yaz'noth hissed.

Yaki's mouth moved but no sound came from it. Pressing her lips together, she nodded.

The dragon's eyes narrowed and the red crystal in Yaki's hands flared back to life. She gasped with a sudden inhalation and coughed.

"But...I won't last a month with this heart. You said so," Yaki wheezed.

"Then you best hurry and get it done. If you die, you'll leave some very pressing unfinished business." Yaz'noth chuckled. "Now swear your oath."

"Don't do it, Yaki!" Ishe shouted. "Give me one more chance, Yaz'noth. I can do as you ask. Let her go."

Yaki looked up, pain and anger dug into her features. "Shut up, Ishe." Tears shone in the corners of her eyes. "You've done enough." She lay back to look up at Yaz'noth. "I swear on my mother's name that I will bring you this quicksilver."

"Good enough." His victorious grin shone like polished mirrors in the morning sun. "Your ride will be here in three hours." Yaz'noth shifted his gaze to Ishe, and the smile turned sly. "You and I will be spending a lot of quality time together. I've been reading about the most interesting human syndrome. I wonder if I can induce it."

Yaki and Ishe will return in Dragon's Birth on March 31st!
Click here to preorder!

The Seven Saved Lands

To The Federated Cities

Lundon

Grave Of The Fox Fine

Two Rivers Tribal Nation

Buffalo Plains

Valhalla

City Proper

High Tree

The Golden Hills

The Night's Hidden Valley

Wolf Rider Territory

Lair Of The White Queen

The Wilding Wastes

The Drowned Coast

A Note from the Author

I have so many people who have helped me with constructing this series that its going to take quite a few words to get through them all. Let me start with you, my reader, thank you for reading and enjoying Dragon's Price. You are ultimately the reason I commit my thoughts to digital ink and then spend months sawing and hacking at them until they resemble something more coherent than the mad gibberings that are my rough drafts. The Rise of the Horned Serpent started as a simple idea, Sky Pirates vs. Dragons and has grown wildly out of control with ideas and creatures that make me cackle with glee. Thank you for riding along, enjoying these sights, and helping me continue my scribblings.

Beyond you, Amanda Potter, my awesome wife deserves a fortune of happy tidings and her weight in gold for helping me throughout the process of bringing this story to life. She has served as everything from chief idea bouncer off-er, plot therapist, cheerleader to content editor, alpha reader, graphic design and typesetter. She had a hand in every part of this book and it would not have happened without her.

Thank you to the many others beta readers who also gave me advice along the way: Megan Haskell, Alec Hutson, Megan Marsh, Rachel Bailey, Jennifer Holbrook, and Sarah Craft.

And thank you to my Patreons: AC Cobble, Baylong Feuer, Bryce O'Connor, Chandra, Denis Trenque, Foe, Jixstun, John Yewell, Matt Moss, Megan Haskell, T L Greylock and Timandra Whitecastle for all the encouragement and support you give me every month.

facebook.com/FallenKittenProductions

twitter.com/fallenkittenpro

Also by Daniel Potter

Freelance Familiars Series

Off Leash

Marking Territory

High Steaks

Scales & Sky: Rise of the Horned Serpent

Dragon's Price

Dragon's Cage (coming March 2019)

Dragon's Run (coming soon)

Dragon's Siege (coming soon)

Made in the USA
Middletown, DE
10 April 2019